Nothing, Everything, Nothing

Casia Schreyer

This is a work of fiction. Names, characters, places, and incidents either are the creation of the author or used fictitiously and any resemblance to actual persons, living or dead, business establishments, events, or locales is entirely coincidental.

NOTHING, EVERYTHING, NOTHING

Copyright ©2014 by Casia Schreyer
E-book edition released 2014
Paperback edition released 2014

Cover Photography by Evan Wilman
Cover Design by Casia Schreyer

All rights reserved.
No part of this book may be reproduced, scanned, or distributed in any printed or electronic form without permission. Please do not participate in or encourage the piracy of copyrighted materials.

ISBN: 978-1502972989

Distributed by Amazon Online Retailer, CreatSpace E-Store, Smashwords E-Store

This book is dedicated to my cousin
Marlee
Your story isn't over

And for all teens and adults battling depression
You are not alone
Your story isn't over

Author's Note

In my defense, I started this novel two months before Robin Williams killed himself. I started this as a way to feel like I was doing something because there was nothing I could do to help my cousin who was (and is) battling depression and suicide. Now everyone is talking about it – and talking is good.

Depression is a serious thing. Don't mistake it for teen angst, teen drama, a cry for attention, or a temporary sadness. All these exist, of course, and they pass. But depression is serious. Real, mind numbing, body numbing, depression is serious.

Suicide is also serious and though often linked with depression that isn't always the case. Certain medications and mental health issues can lead to suicidal thoughts. Teenagers with no one to support them are also at risk.

There are resources out there, here are a few:

Mayo Clinic: http://www.mayoclinic.org/diseases-conditions/suicide/in-depth/suicide/art-20044707

Psych Central: http://www.metanoia.org/suicide/whattodo.htm

Psych Central: http://psychcentral.com/lib/what-to-do-when-you-think-someone-is-suicidal/0007461

Psychology Today: http://www.psychologytoday.com/blog/promoting-hope-preventing-suicide/201201/5-dos-when-someone-says-im-suicidal

Suicide.org: http://www.suicide.org/how-to-help-a-suicidal-person.html

National Suicide Prevention Hotline: 1-800-273-TALK (8255) http://www.suicidepreventionlifeline.org/gethelp/someone.aspx

Kids Help Phone: 1-800-668-6868 http://org.kidshelpphone.ca/en

Please use only reliable sources for advice when dealing with suicide prevention. See a school counsellor, physician, psychologist, or psychiatrist, if you, or someone you know, is experiencing suicidal thoughts.

If someone comes to you and tells you they are thinking of committing suicide do not brush them aside, do not think they are joking, and do not panic. Do what you can to talk to them and get them help. If you think they will commit suicide within the next day or two take them to a hospital ER before it happens. The hospital has access to a lot of resources.

These people are stronger than you can imagine, and if they're coming to you for help it means they trust you, and they NEED help.

This novel is about a young girl who becomes suicidal. She is caught up in a toxic situation that has made her blind to the positive people in her life. Many teens and parents of teens provided stories and anecdotes which inspired this story. It is fiction but it is built on a scary truth. This truth is more common than most people imagine.

I refer to Facebook quite often in this novella. This is my disclaimer:

Facebook can be a very useful site for networking and for keeping in touch with family and friends. I use Facebook all the time. Facebook is not responsible for teens committing suicide and I am not implying that at any time in this book. What's that saying? "Guns don't kill people, people kill people." Facebook doesn't drive teens to suicide. It is unfortunate that some people have twisted social media into a platform for bullying but that is their own doing, not a flaw in Social Media.

Facebook is owned by someone who is not me. I don't own the name or any rights to it. Neither do I own Twitter or any other brand, store, or site named in this story, or rights to the names or content.

This book would not have been completed without the help of a lot of people. First, and foremost, is Andreas Ganz, my beta reader. When I handed him the first attempt he said, "You've given me an outline! I want to know all about these people and their lives and how they came to this situation. Give me more!" So it was back to the drawing board and the story was expanded by two weeks with over a dozen scenes added.

Second, the original inspiration came from my cousin who hit a rough patch. She's not the only person I've known who has brushed against suicide but she's my goddaughter and I love her very much. In addition, I drew inspiration from the cases of Amanda Todd and Megan Meier.

Third is the National Novel Writing Month Facebook Group, which we lovingly refer to as the Nano Hive-mind. This wonderful group of writers helped me rework difficult passages, polish the summaries and blurbs, and get inside the mentality of a modern teenagers (I'm not old but the cellphone I had in high school is nothing like the smart phones kids have today). They also helped me delve into the darkness of suicide so that this portrayal could be accurate and compassionate.

While Andy read the book to help me solidify the plot, my grandmother, Thea Clincke, was busy reading the manuscript for spelling mistakes, grammatical errors, and misused words. She has been helping kids with homework for going on 45 years and for someone who learned English at 16 she's very good at it. She proof reads many of my stories.

Last but never least is my husband, Jonathan. He is infinitely patient with me when I approach a creative deadline and the chores fall by the wayside. He watches the kids while I write and edit. He washes dishes and folds laundry. I'm blessed to have him supporting me.

CHAPTER 1

Molly really wasn't surprised that she and her sister were arguing. It was Spring Break across the city and that meant both she and Shannon were home every day. It was only Sunday, not even really Spring Break yet, but already they were grating on each other's nerves. "It's my laptop," Molly said again, blocking the doorway into her bedroom, her only safe haven.

Eight-year-old Shannon stomped her foot, "Mom told me to use it! She's busy paying bills and doing her work on the computer and I need to do my homework!"

"MOM! It's my laptop! Stop telling Shannon she can use it!"

"You're going out, you don't need it!" their mom called back.

"It's my laptop!"

"But I paid for it." Their mom stuck her head around the corner and glared. "Really Molly, it's not like she's trying to snoop through your files. She just needs to do some research."

"She has a week."

Mother and teenager stared at each other.

Finally Molly said, "I don't want her in my room."

"That's the beauty of a laptop, it moves."

"Then I'll take it with me."

"To the pool? Molly, you're being ridiculous."

A car horn honked outside a moment before someone rang the doorbell.

Molly didn't move. The doorbell rang again.

"Are you going to get the door? It's probably Kirsten here to pick you up."

The doorbell rang again, this time twice in rapid succession.

"Fine. I'm going. But I don't want her in my room!" Molly grabbed her bag and the laptop and stormed down the hallway. She left the laptop in the living room and opened the door as Kirsten was about to ring again. "Let's get out of here." She slammed the door shut behind her without calling good-bye.

"Rough morning?" Kirsten asked as they walked down to the car. Two other girls were waiting in the front seats with the radio blaring.

"The worst. You're lucky you don't have a sister."

"Aww. I think Shannon's cute."

"Yeah, until she wants to go in your room and use your computer," Molly said as she and Kirsten climbed in the back seat.

"That's rough," said Julie from the driver's seat. She pulled away from the curb. "Tell her off, I totally would. It's your space and your laptop."

"I tried, believe me. My mom got involved. She said she paid for the laptop so Shannon's allowed to use it."

"Buy your own," Kirsten said.

"With what money?"

"Don't you get allowance?"

Molly rolled her eyes. "Sure, but it's barely enough for lunch every day. There's no way I'm bringing sandwiches to school. I'd look like a total dork!"

Kirsten smiled thinly and patted Molly's leg. "Honey, between you and me, it might not be a bad idea to cut back on those lunches. There's nothing wrong with curves, boys like curves, but at some point curves become rolls and *no one* finds rolls attractive."

Molly looked at Kirsten in her size 0 short-shorts and extra small crop-top then down at her own outfit of knee length shorts and over-sized t-shirt. She knew the tag on the back of her shorts didn't read anything close to "0". "Do you think I'm getting fat?"

"No sweetie," Kirsten said. "I just want you to be careful. You don't want to end up fat and alone, do you?"

Molly shook her head and turned to stare out the window. She knew she was the largest in her group of friends and for all she knew it was her eating habits that had caused it. Her mother was petite and pretty. She didn't know her father but since her step-dad, Hank, was a wiry man she couldn't imagine her mom hooking up with a fat man at any time in her past.

"Aw, don't worry about it Molly," cooed Kirsten. "We still love you."

The pool was crowded with teenagers looking for a cheap place to hang out. It wasn't hot yet but most of the teens in town had spent the previous at the mall and had already taken advantage of all the sales and most of the other entertainment, like movies, didn't start until late afternoon or evening.

Molly changed in one of the bathroom stalls, adjusting the straps and leg edges of her one-piece sports-style bathing suit before coming out. She paused in front of the mirror to check her hair, which was shaved on one side and bright blue on the other, and sighed. *I'm curvy all right, curvy in all the wrong places.* Clutching her clothes to her chest she scurried to the lockers and swapped her clothes for a towel.

The other girls were tucking their clothes away too, each in a lovely string bikini. They were almost exact copies of each other, except for their hair colour and the colour of their bathing suits. *And I'm the ugly duckling,* Molly thought.

"Ready?" Kirsten said, smiling.

Behind her Julie and Amanda snickered.

"Yeah, I'm ready."

Out in the pool area they spotted a large group of kids from their school and Molly was dragged in their direction. The other girls struck up conversations instantly leaving Molly hanging back. One boy with neat, short, cinnamon coloured hair approached her.

"Hey Molly, I didn't know you were coming today. How's life?"

Molly smiled but said, "Hi, Brandon, life sucks, like always. Who'd you come with?"

"My mom dropped me off. I didn't realize this was going to be the hottest hang-out place."

One of the other guys in the group walked by, going out of his way to elbow Brandon as he passed. Brandon flinched and tried to smile.

"Uh, you want to hop in the pool?"

Before Molly could answer Brandon her friends reappeared. "Come on Molly, we're going to sit in the hot tub," Kirsten said, grabbing her arm.

Amanda and Julie eyed Brandon with open superiority.

Brandon trailed along. "It's so hot outside, why do you want to go in the hot tub?"

"Well, if it's too hot for you, get lost," Julie snapped. Amanda giggled.

Brandon stopped short and stared at Molly and her friends. Molly glanced over her shoulder, an apologetic smile on her face, and then a group of middle-graders passed between them, aiming for the pool.

"Didn't I warn you?" Kirsten said.

"Warn me about what?" Molly hated the hot tub but she slid in beside her friends anyways.

"You've got to watch your weight or the only guys who will pay attention to you are the losers." Kirsten sunk lower with a sigh.

"Brandon's not a loser," Molly said. The other girls just stared at her until she blushed. "I mean, he's not cool or anything either …"

Amanda snickered. "You can do so much better. Just look at that."

They all turned their attention to the boy who had just climbed out of the pool. His dark hair was boy-band long and dripping. He was grinning as he waved at some friends across the room paying no attention to the quartet of admirers in the hot tub.

"Look at his muscles," Julie sighed.

"Who is he?" Molly asked.

"That's Lance," Kirsten said smugly. "He's a senior."

"He goes to our school? I've never seen him before," Amanda said.

Julie gave her a shove. "As if you know everybody."

"I know everybody important," Amanda shot back.

"Apparently not."

Kirsten rolled her eyes. "Oh, knock it off, both of you. He transferred, or moved, or something. He just showed up in my brother's class a month ago." She settled lower again and closed her eyes.

Molly was bored already. The hot tub was too hot and crowded with people she didn't know and her friends were relaxing and not talking. *And if they do start talking they might start talking about how fat I am again and then everyone will start looking at me. I hate it when people stare at me.*

Molly was staring sullenly at the pool, only half paying attention, so she was just as surprised as her friends when a deep voice said, "Do you ladies mind if I join you?"

Lance was halfway down the steps into the hot tub. He smiled at them and Molly felt her heart do a flip-flop. She swallowed hard, unable to speak.

Kirsten didn't have that problem. She flashed an impossibly bright smile and sat up taller so her breasts were just visible over the top of the water. "Of course you're welcome to sit with us. Come on in."

"How's your brother doing, Kirsten?"

"He hates his job but loves the money."

Lance laughed and Molly's heart did another flip-flop. "Life's a bitch." His smile turned from friendly to flirty as he turned to the other girls. "I'm Lance, by the way."

"Julie."

"And I'm Amanda."

Both girls scooted to the edges of their benches, smiling wide.

Lance's attention skimmed over them and settled on Molly. "And you, Cutie?"

"Oh." She swallowed hard. "Molly. I'm Molly."

Lance slid through the water and settled between Molly and Kirsten but his attention remained focused on Molly. "Molly. That's a really nice name. Does it mean something?"

"I … I don't know. It was my mom's aunt's name." Molly shrugged. "She died just before I was born."

"Well, it's still pretty, like you."

Kirsten frowned at Julie and Amanda and slid closer to Lance. "I guess you're pretty excited about graduating. It's all my brother can talk about. He's not seeing anyone so he's trying to find someone to take to prom."

Lance shrugged but didn't take his eyes off Molly's face. "I guess so. I don't think about it too much. I try to live in the here and now."

"That's so … so … deep," Amanda said.

"Well, I only came in because the pool will feel even colder when I jump back in." He stood, the water only coming up to his waist now.

Molly could feel her cheeks burning and she tried to find somewhere to look that wouldn't embarrass her. A hand entered her field of vision and she looked up at him.

"Did you want to come?"

She nodded and let him help her up. Kirsten, Julie, and Amanda exchanged glances and scurried after them.

Molly plunged into the water. Even though it was freezing she stayed under as long as she could. When she came up gasping for air Lance was busy chasing Kirsten, Julie, and Amanda around the pool. Treading water she took a deep breath and tried to relax.

Behind her someone yelled, "Head's up!" and then there was a splash beside her. Brandon popped out of the water, spluttering and shaking water from his face. "Hello again."

Molly tried to smile but she looked over her shoulder toward Lance, just in case he was looking. He wasn't so Molly said, "Hey Brandon."

"Having fun?"

"I guess so."

"Did you want to leave? We could go hang somewhere else, somewhere with fewer people."

"Oh. I don't know about that."

Brandon studied her a moment. "Why not? If you're worried about getting home you know my mom would drive you."

Molly shook her head. "It's not that."

He sighed. "Did you want me to leave you alone so you can be cool?"

Before Molly could answer Lance swam over. "Aren't you going to join us?" he said with a smile that made her heart try to break her ribs.

"Yes. I'm coming." Without a backward glance she swam after Lance.

When Molly disappeared into the changing stall Julie took a deep breath and said, "Can you believe Lance was paying attention to her? What could he possibly see in her?"

"Maybe he likes big girls," Amanda said.

"Maybe we could find out," Kirsten said. "Lance and my brother started gaming together just after Lance transferred to our school a few months ago."

"You're so lucky," Julie sighed.

"Oh he's never paid any real attention to me before. We'll set something up for today, see her reaction, and his, and maybe get some answers."

Julie and Amanda grinned and Julie said, "Sounds like the perfect plan."

Molly came out of the change room toweling the long side of her hair dry. Her friends were huddled together on the bench whispering back and forth. "What's going on guys?" Molly said.

"Oh, we were just discussing your turn of luck," Julie said.

"Yeah, how you upgraded from Brandon to Lance in one afternoon is … well … surprising," said Amanda.

"But I didn't …" Molly started.

Kirsten rolled her eyes. "You girls are just jealous. Let's get moving. The day's a wasting."

"Can you drop me off at home?" Molly said. "My mom said 'only a few hours' and it has been a few hours. She'll get mad if I stay out late."

Now it was Julie's turn to roll her eyes. "Fine. But you'll miss all the fun. We're going to Kirsten's house."

Amanda giggled. "Kirsten's going to talk her brother into calling Lance over for some guy time."

"Lance will be there?"

Kirsten nodded. "Are you sure you won't come?"

Molly's heart was pounding hard. "Yeah. I'll come," she said, hoping her anticipation didn't show.

As soon as they got to Kirsten's house Molly said, "Can I use the phone?"

"Of course," said Kirsten. "Use the one in the kitchen. We'll just be waiting in the living room."

They all smiled at her and waited for her to walk out and then their smiles dropped away. "Let's go," Kirsten said.

In the living room they settled all together on one couch and kept their voices hushed. "I texted my brother while we were in the car."

"So Lance is coming?" Julie asked.

"Yeah, he's coming. And my brother ordered pizza for us. After Molly is gone we'll corner Lance and get the low down on the situation."

Julie huffed. "Pooh. I have to drive Molly home. I'll miss it."

"We'll tell you all about it," Amanda said, patting her friend's leg.

Molly sat in Kirsten's kitchen with the phone to her ear while her mother ranted and lectured. "It's just Kirsten's house," Molly interjected.

"It's not what we agreed on, Molly. You said you were going to the pool and coming home. Your aunt is coming over this evening, you knew that."

"Mom, it's just one evening. Kirsten's mom is cool with us being over. We won't be here super late. And Julie will give me a lift home."

"Like she was supposed to give you a lift home after swimming?"

"Mom! Why is this such a big deal? Amanda's mom and Julie's mom were both okay with the change of plans!"

"Well, since your step-dad has the car I can't come pick you up so I guess you're staying there until Julie drives you home. But Hank will be home at 9pm so if you're not here by 9:30 I'm coming to get you."

"Okay, okay. I'll tell Julie."

"And you're welcome."

"Fine, whatever. I'll see you later." Molly hung up the phone as her friends came in, sharp smiles on their faces.

"Are we good?" Kirsten asked.

"All cool," Molly said, shoving aside the guilt that threatened to well up inside her. "But my mom wants me home by 9:30."

"Sure," said Julie. "No problem."

"Is Lance coming?"

"He's on his way," Kirsten said. "Let's crash downstairs until he gets here."

Kirsten's basement had a giant television hooked to two gaming consoles and a huge sectional sofa. The girls settled in to gossip and just hang-out, the way they often did in the evenings and on the weekends.

"My waist line is going to hate the pizza," Kirsten said. "I'm going to be throwing up all night, I just know it."

"Are you still purging?" Julie asked, frowning. "I thought you were going to stop that."

"I was. But last week my jeans were snug so I thought, just once or twice more, just to stay in shape. Of course the pizza tonight is a horrible idea." She rested a hand on her stomach. "Ugh, pizza makes me feel bloated."

"Then don't eat it," Amanda said. "Order a salad."

Kirsten rolled her eyes. "Boys like a girl with healthy appetites; they just don't like looking at her afterwards. It's like they don't understand how quickly a slice of pizza goes to our thighs. Right Molly?"

Molly forced a thin smile. "Right, of course."

The doorbell rang and Amanda squealed. "He's here!"

Kirsten rolled her eyes but Molly felt her chest tighten. "Excuse me. I need the bathroom." She bolted across the basement and locked herself in the bathroom. She sank to the floor, her back against the door. The unfinished cement was cool under her hands. Alone she could feel herself beginning to relax again. Over the sound of the fan she could hear hushed female voices punctuated by giggles and shushing.

Male voices joined in and all sense of calm vanished. It became hard to breathe and the bathroom suddenly made her feel claustrophobic.

I have to get out of here, she thought. *But Lance is out there. I can't go out there. Why did I agree to this!?*

She could feel tears springing to her eyes. Years ago she used to hyperventilate if she cried too hard so her mom had taught her how to calm down with controlled breathing. Now she squeezed her eyes shut tight and focused on what her mom had taught her.

Breathe in. *You're okay.*

Breathe out. *This is no big deal.*

Breathe in. *Kirsten and Julie and Amanda are here.*

Breathe out. *It's just a hang out.*

She opened her eyes again. She swallowed hard and rose shakily to her feet. She went to the sink and washed her hands and splashed water on her face. She flushed the toilet and paused in front of the door. She straightened her shirt, took a deep breath, and tried to smile.

Everyone was staring at her when she opened the door and she had the sudden urge to slam it shut again. Instead she turned the light off and took an uncertain step into the room.

"Did you get lost in there?" Julie said.

Molly blinked a few times, startled. "I ... uh ..."

Lance turned a serious face towards Julie. "Did you just turn seven? What do you care what she was doing in the bathroom?"

Molly's friends exchanged glances and Julie stammered, "I ... she was just ... it's not like ... it was just a joke."

Kirsten was glaring at her. Kirsten's brother, Trevor, was watching from the stairs and smirking. Julie looked like she was going to die from embarrassment. Only Amanda's attention flitted from one person to the next as she waited to see what would happen.

And it's all because of me, Molly thought.

"It's okay," Molly said quickly. "I knew she was joking. I just didn't have a good comeback is all." She tried to walk calmly across the room but she knew her steps were hurried. Sitting on the couch with Julie and Amanda was out of the question since Julie looked like she might take the time to kill her before dying of embarrassment and Kirsten was still glaring which left only the rocking chair in the corner. Molly dropped into it hating the way the old wooden joints creaked.

Kirsten's brother said, "Let's go, I have the computers set up and the guys are waiting to game."

"Yeah. Bye girls, bye Molly."

The doorbell rang again and Kirsten's brother yelled, "I'll get it but you have to come up and get the pizza yourselves!"

The other girls bolted off the couches and up the stairs, quickly catching up to Lance. Molly just sat staring at the tacky carpet. She didn't understand Julie's reaction. She didn't know what to think of Kirsten purging, or why she hadn't heard about it before. And she didn't know why Lance was singling her out when her friends were slender and pretty and she was just plain fat.

"Are you coming?" Kirsten called down the stairs.

"Yeah, I'm coming," Molly called back. The chair creaked again as she stood up. Even though she was starving she took only one slice of pizza and turned down her favourite pop in favour of water.

Kirsten eyed her for a moment. "Come on, I ordered all this food and that's all you're going to eat."

"I'm not really hungry," she lied and tried to disappear into the corner.

Kirsten rolled her eyes and the conversation moved on but Molly was too nervous to really pay much attention.

The ride home was even worse than dinner. Amanda was being picked up later and of course Kirsten didn't need a ride home so it was just Julie and Molly in the car. The radio was on but instead of breaking the silence it only made Molly more aware that they weren't talking or laughing together.

There was a train at the only set of tracks they had to cross, the tracks that divided the old suburb, filled with outdated bungalows and block after block of duplexes and town houses, from the newer housing development with its cookie-cutter split levels and attached garages.

"Why are you mad at me?" Molly blurted out as the train cars rumbled by.

Julie glanced at her then back at the train. "Who said I was mad at you?"

"At Kirsten's, you snapped at me."

"Oh grow up, Molly. I told you, it was just a joke."

"Oh."

"Look, I'm not in the mood for any touchy feely stuff, okay? If your feelings are hurt go cry to someone else. I didn't do anything wrong."

As they pulled up to the curb Molly could see tail lights backing down her driveway. As she stepped out the tail lights stopped and a moment later her mom was standing on the driveway next to Hank's car.

"Where were you? I was just coming to get you."

With the car door still open Molly could hear Julie snickering behind her. "The clock in Julie's car says 9:30 so I'm on time. Besides, we got stopped by a train or we'd have been here five minutes ago." She leaned down. "Thanks for the ride."

Julie gave her a pained smile and put the car back in gear. As she pulled away Molly was left alone with her mother.

"You know I worry about you," her mom said. "I know you want freedom right now but you're only sixteen. I'm trying to give you room to grow even though it's hard for me to let go but you need to respect the rules."

"I know." She kicked at a tuft of grass. "Am I in trouble?"

"No. The train wasn't your fault." She held out an arm to her daughter. "Come on."

Molly let her mother wrap an arm over her shoulders and lead her into the house.

"Did you have fun today?"

"Yeah, of course," Molly said.

"Brandon called."

Molly just nodded.

"He mentioned there was an older boy hanging around with you at the pool."

"He wasn't hanging around with just me."

"Who is he?"

"A friend of Kirsten's brother."

Her mother frowned. "Is that why you went to Kirsten's house?"

Molly shrugged off her mom's arm and huffed. "No. We barely saw him. He was playing computer games with Kirsten's brother. We just wanted to hang out and have some pizza."

"Okay, I'm sorry."

"What did Brandon want?"

"His mom has some extra rhubarb. He wanted to know if I wanted some, and to talk to you. He was disappointed that you weren't home."

"I saw him at the pool. I don't need to hang out with him all the time."

"You used to hang out with him all the time."

"Things change, okay. I have Kirsten and Julie and Amanda now."

Her mom nodded. "Just don't burn any bridges, okay?"

"Yeah, whatever."

After Julie and Molly left Kirsten and Amanda crashed in the computer room with the guys. They were halfway through a match in some sword-and-sorcery, real-time, online game that Kirsten and Amanda had zero interest in. As soon as the match was over the guys excused themselves from the group and logged off.

"Okay, Kirsten, what's going on?" Trevor asked.

"What do you mean?" Kirsten said, smiling sweetly.

"You never come in here while I'm gaming. You think computer games are dumb."

Kirsten turned her smile, and attention, to Lance. "We wanted to talk to Lance about our run-in at the pool today."

"What about it?" Lance said. "We hung out." He shrugged.

"You seemed awfully fond of Molly," Amanda blurted out and then blushed.

Kirsten rolled her eyes. "So much for subtle."

Trevor chuckled but said nothing.

"You want to know why?"

The girls nodded their eyes wide and eager.

"Molly interests me. I think I might want to ask her out, if you two thought she'd say yes that is."

"She'd be stupid to say no," Amanda said.

Lance turned to Kirsten. "Don't frown, it'll give you wrinkles."

"Why her?" Kirsten asked.

"Why not her? Are you jealous?"

"No," Kirsten lied, adding a huff of indignation for good measure. "Are you one of those chubby chasers?"

Lance laughed. "She's not fat enough to catch the eye of a real chubby chaser, and no, that's not why. Look, I can tell she's not as popular as you three, I can tell she's worried about her self-image, and I can tell you only let her hang around with you to make you three look better. If you're not jealous, why do you care?"

"She is our friend," Kirsten said with more false indignation. "You don't have to be skinny to have friends."

"Right, that's why Julie treats her so badly, because you're friends. I'm not an idiot Kirsten and I'm a very good reader of people. Molly is naïve and insecure and exactly the type of girl I'm looking for. You don't need to know why. And if you really are her friends you'll be happy that a boy is showing interest in her."

Kirsten's frown deepened before she could stop it. "Fine, but don't expect us to help you with whatever you're up to."

"You don't trust me?" he asked.

"No."

"We don't?" Amanda squeaked.

"Come on Amanda. Julie should be home soon. She'll want a full report."

In Kirsten's room they called up Julie, setting Kirsten's cell to speaker phone and flopping on the bed.

"I don't treat her badly," Julie huffed as Kirsten told her about the conversation with Lance. "It's just friendly banter. It's not my fault that Molly can't take a joke."

"Well we know that," Kirsten said, rolling her eyes. "What we don't know is why Lance is interested in Molly. She can't flirt, she's not that pretty, she's on the large side, she's socially awkward …"

"I'm still wondering why you let her hang out with us this year," Julie said. "You knew all that when you invited her to that hang-out in September. She's only been trying to be friends with us since ninth grade, the needy little …"

"Julie, you can't be popular if people don't like you," Kirsten said.

Julie sighed. "But couldn't we find adoring fans that are actually interesting to be around?"

"That would be beside the point. They're supposed to be interested in us, not the other way around. And the boys are supposed to be interested in us too."

Amanda propped herself up on an elbow. "I think it's sweet. Molly will be so happy to be the center of attention."

Kirsten glared at Amanda until the girl blushed and looked away. "Well, if Lance wants to make Molly the center of attention so will we."

"I thought we weren't going to help Lance," Amanda said, confused.

"What do you have in mind, Kirsten?" Julie said.

"Oh, nothing much, we'll just pay attention to *everything* about Molly so that Lance sees just how awkward she is and will stop paying attention to her."

"I don't want to pay attention to Molly," Julie snapped. "I don't even like her being a part of the group."

Kirsten rolled her eyes. "Then we'll drift away from her over the summer. Until then, let's make sure everyone knows she's less than we are, and that we're just so kind to make her a part of our group."

CHAPTER 2

Molly didn't have cool toys like the video game system and rock star game but she had a bigger house so when she and Brandon wanted to hang out he brought his cool toys to her house for the afternoon. Brandon's mom, Barb, and Molly's mom, Joanna, who was never called Jo or Anna, had been best friends since high school. The two women met often for coffee which meant Brandon's toys saw a lot of travel.

Molly put down the guitar shaped controller and stretched. It was a perfect day; no stress, no younger sister, no pretenses. Brandon grinned at her. "Did you want to play again?" he asked.

Molly shook her head, smiling back at him. "Maybe later. I bet our moms have a snack on the table by now."

"Well then, what are we waiting for?" Brandon was off the couch like a shot leaving Molly to scramble up the stairs after him.

Molly and Brandon had been friends all their lives and until recently Brandon would have said they were best friends. Things like friendship shifted so easily in high school.

Today Joanna and Barb were sitting in the kitchen with their coffee and a box of donuts Joanna had picked up on her way back from dropping her Shannon off at a play date and had hidden in the back of the fridge. The two teenagers skidded into the kitchen and grinned.

"It's like they can smell the food, even from the basement," Joanna said, holding out the flimsy carton.

Molly took a chocolate donut with chocolate icing and Brandon grabbed the apple cruller. They snagged two cans of pop from the fridge and disappeared. A moment later Barb and Joanna could hear music coming from the basement.

Joanna shook her head and stared into her coffee for a moment, her smile gone. "You know, I'm having trouble letting her grow up. What if they turn out like us?"

Barb laughed. "You mean happily working at jobs they enjoy? Look at us, Joanna. You're a freelance webpage designer and I'm an accountant. We pay our bills on time, we spoil our kids ..."

"We were pregnant at 18, I was homeless..."

"Homeless! You were never homeless."

"That's what they call it when your parents kick you out, Barb. I know I wasn't homeless long."

"You were homeless for all of thirty seconds. We had fun living together and raising those two together, even if it was only for a few months."

"Yeah, those were good months." Joanna sighed. "It's not that I regret it, but I hope Molly makes better decisions that I did."

Downstairs Molly and Brandon were sprawled on the couches with their snacks. "This is fun," Molly said. "What other games do you have?"

"None that can have two players, not yet anyways" Brandon replied around a mouth full of cruller. "You know, I've sort of missed spending time with you."

Molly chuckled but Brandon could tell that it wasn't as carefree as normal. "You and your mom are here, what? Once-a-month at least. And I saw you at the pool yesterday."

"But I didn't get to spend time with you at the pool and I don't see you at school anymore, not since you started hanging out with Kaitlyn."

"Her name is Kirsten." Molly sighed. "Yeah, I know I haven't been spending a lot of time with you outside of our one class together, I'm sorry about that. But that happens in life, right? Friendships sort of shift sometimes and it's not like we're not still friends."

Brandon nodded. "Did you want to play another song?"

"We've played every song we know, some of them twice!" Molly laughed.

"What about this one?" Brandon said, pausing on a title. "It's easy to play and it's a fun song."

"I've never heard of it," Molly said.

"My mom says it was on the radio when she was in high school," Brandon said with a shrug.

Molly laughed. "So it's as old as we are?"

"Probably older, but not by much." Brandon selected the song and they waited for it to load. By the time Barb called down the stairs for Brandon so they could head for home Molly and Brandon had played every song on the game at least once.

Molly used to like Spring Break; it was a little taste of vacation tucked between Christmas and summer that was as refreshing as the steadily warming weather. She was one of the lucky kids who had a parent home full time so she always got to have friends over for sleepovers and go out for lunch with her mom. Over the last few years her sentiments had slowly changed. Lunch out with Mom lost its appeal and she was envious of other kids who got to stay home alone all day, watching any movies they liked, sleeping in late every day, and eating junk food at all hours. She was still allowed to have friends over, but Brandon was the only one who didn't tease her about her mom's hovering.

After a few boring days at home helping with the housework Molly had called Kirsten to come and hang out. Brandon had taken his game system home with him so there wasn't much to do aside from flipping channels on the television or watching music videos on Molly's laptop. It was just as well because Molly wasn't sure Kirsten would enjoy video games. Since all the Spring Break specials were aimed at twelve year olds and the soap operas and talk shows were boring the two girls were sprawled on Molly's bed reading the stack of magazines Kirsten had brought over while listening to a music video playlist.

Kirsten was absorbed in the most recent edition of her favourite teen magazine and she kept showing Molly snippets of articles and interviews. Molly just flipped through older issues with a passing interest while wishing that she had picked the music.

The song changed and Kirsten sat bolt upright. "Oh my gosh, this is just the greatest song on the radio right now!"

Molly had heard the song a few times but had barely noticed it, except to note that it wasn't really her style. Now she smiled big and said, "I know I just can't listen to it enough."

Kirsten tossed her magazine on the pile and turned to Molly with a conspiratorial grin on her face. "Want me to do you make-up?"

Molly hesitated. "I don't have a lot of make-up, and besides, it's not like we're going anywhere today."

"Going out has nothing to do with it, Molly. We just want you to look your best. We care about you, Molly, and we want people to like you."

"You like me, and so does Julie and Amanda and ... well, you guys like me," Molly said, deliberately leaving Brandon off the list. Molly had been trying to make friends with Kirsten, Julie, and Amanda for two years before they finally accepted her into their tight-knit group that fall. She didn't want to do anything to jeopardize that friendship.

"Of course we like you, Hun, but what about Lance? You want him to like you, right?"

Molly hadn't given much thought to dating, not even after Lance had flirted with her at the pool, but it was the only thing her new friends seemed to think about so she said, "Of course I do."

"Well then we have to see about getting you some better make-up."

"With what money?" Molly said again. It was a sore point for her, and another difference between her and her friends. They all lived in nice houses and their parents had great jobs. Molly lived in a duplex and her step-father loaded trailers for a living. At least her mom's job was cool, but being a freelance web designer didn't exactly pay out gold and diamonds.

"Fine, show me what you have and I'll try to work with it."

As Kirsten worked Molly thought about how different she was from her friends. She wanted to be like them, she wanted to be liked by them, but they were slender and athletic with straight hair, Kirsten's in blonde, Julie's in brown, and Amanda's somewhere in between. Molly was curvy, if she felt like being generous, fat if she was feeling down on herself, and her Native-black hair was thick and unruly. Brandon had talked her into shaving the left side and bleaching the right. It suited her, but it made her stand out.

Kirsten stepped back with a triumphant smile and turned Molly towards the mirror.

Molly stared at her face. She didn't recognize herself. Just behind her Kirsten stood grinning. "What do you think?"

Molly took a slow, deep breath and smiled. "You did a really great job."

"Were you paying attention to what I was doing?"

"Of course," Molly lied.

"Good. Now you'll be able to do your own make-up and we'll work on building up your selection. Some new eye-shadow, just to have a variety of colour, some better mascara because yours is no-brand garbage, and …"

There was a knocking at the front door that made Kirsten pause and a moment later Joanna called, "Kirsten, your mom is here."

"Okay, let me just get my stuff from Molly's room," Kirsten called back.

Molly trailed after her friend. "Thanks for coming," she said. "And thanks for the make-up tips."

"Oh, don't mention it. We want you to look your best for Lance, right?" And then Kirsten was gone in a whirl of smiles and blonde hair leaving Molly feeling breathless and disconnected.

CHAPTER 3

Molly stepped off the school bus and let the crowd push her towards the red brick building. She attended one of the larger high schools in the city but compared to the high school her cousin had attended it was still very small even with two gyms.

Even though it was a beautiful spring day she felt grey inside. She didn't like going to class because she felt she wasn't the brightest and the teachers only seemed to ask her questions when she didn't know the answers. She hated other people staring at her and she hated doing school work. What she liked was the hustle and bustle of people, the ever-changing conversations that buzzed around her as she walked down the halls, the feelings of excitement and belonging that surrounded her as long as she could just blend with the crowd, and of course, the chance to hang out with her friends, especially now that she was friends with Kirsten, Julie, and Amanda.

The girls were hanging around the corner where they, and several other girls they occasionally hung out with, had their lockers. They were leaned in close to each other and talking in hushed voices. Molly smiled as soon as she saw them and rushed over to join them.

"Morning!"

They all looked at her and Kirsten held up a hand. "We don't want you to hear this, okay? Just go stash your stuff. We'll talk later."

Molly stopped and someone bumped her shoulder.

"Watch it," said the other student as they kept on going down the hallway. The flow of students shifted around Molly.

"Uh … okay." Hiding her bruised feelings she hurried to her locker. The door opened towards her friends so it hid her face from them. She closed her eyes for a moment while her heart pounded away.

She had never given a second thought to popularity growing up. But then they had graduated from the middle years building to the high school and everything had changed. Two middle-years schools combined in this high school and Molly had met Kirsten.

Kirsten was confident and skinny and pale and blonde, everything Molly wasn't. That Kirsten finally wanted to be her friend was everything to Molly. And she had done everything possible over the school year to stay Kirsten's friend, including cutting most of her ties to Brandon.

Now Kirsten doesn't want to talk to me anymore and I don't even know what I did wrong. They've been upset with me since the swimming pool. Are they mad that Brandon talked to me? I didn't ask him to, I explained that to Kirsten over the break but they've hardly called me all week. Are they upset that I was busy with family the rest of spring break?

The warning bell went off and Molly closed the locker with a sigh. Her friends were already gone.

First period was a Social Issues class. Molly's friends all had Dance first period but Molly had no sense of rhythm and she was too self-conscious to dance in front of other people. She hurried to her spot in the back corner where people couldn't stare at the back of her head and dropped into the chair. Seconds before the bell rang Brandon rushed in and claimed the seat in front of her. It was the only class they had together.

He leaned back. "Hey, are you okay?"

She was tempted to lie, to pretend everything was fine like she did with everyone else, but he wasn't starting at her with empty eyes and he didn't have that 'hurry up I have more important things to do' look on his face.

"I think the girls are mad at me and I have no idea why. I don't think they like me anymore."

"Sucks to be them." When Molly didn't smile Brandon added, "Don't worry, it'll all blow over. You'll see."

Molly shrugged. "Maybe. I hope you're right."

The teacher came in. "Okay everyone, stand up for the anthem."

Molly's mind wandered as the recording of last year's band class playing the national anthem was played over the PA system. She missed all the morning announcements because she was replaying the events of Spring Break over in her mind trying to figure out what she had done wrong.

The teacher's voice was not as easily dismissed, especially when Brandon dropped a stapled packet of papers over his shoulder onto her desk.

"This will be the final big assignment of the year. The presentation of this project will be half of your final exam. This is a big chunk of marks and you'll be working on it at least once per week in class, more as we get closer to the deadline. We have one quick unit to finish and then this project will take over all our time.

"There are many issues facing teens today, as you should all know since you're all teens. In partners, and I do mean groups of two and ONLY groups of two, you'll explore one of those issues. You get to pick your issue. This booklet is for recording research sources, outlining your data and presentation, and so you keep on track with the requirements. Yes, you have to hand this booklet in for marks, no, I'm not printing off extra copies, and yes both partners must hand in their own. Any questions so far?"

He waited but no hands went up.

"Okay. In addition to this booklet you must hand in one report, the page and reference requirements are on the first page of your booklet. Yes, you can e-mail me the finished report; you don't have to print it. The report is a formal look at the statistics and other research you've gathered. The last part of this project is the presentation. You'll be presenting in front of the class. You should take up 15 to 20 minutes, no shorter, no longer. We have a lot of presentations to get through. This is your chance to share not only the statistics but your passion about the subject. Slideshows, old school presentation boards, and videos are all permitted. You hand them in on the due date so I can review them and you present them to the class on the scheduled date. And yes, you will still be expected to speak in front of the class even if you provide a video. Any questions yet?"

A hand in the front row and the girl said, "What sort of topics can we choose from?"

"Good question. Let's brainstorm."

Molly tuned out again, flipping idly through her package of papers, when the teacher suddenly called her name.

"Molly, anything to add?"

"Social pressures," she said without thinking.

The teacher cocked his head. "You mean peer pressure?"

"Yeah; peer-pressure and media pressure." She stopped as kids turned to look at her. "That sort of thing."

"Good ideas, Molly. Thanks." He turned and added them to the list on the smart board. "Anyone else?"

Molly sank lower in her chair and hid behind her papers.

She tuned the class out until the teacher said, "Okay, everybody find a partner and pick a topic. It's first come, first served and I'd like to see each pair do a different topic."

"Can we do a project on porn?" someone shouted.

"No. You're too young to access all the research materials, but nice try."

Brandon turned around. "Did you want to work together?"

Molly shrugged. "I guess so."

"I know your friends don't like me, but you did say we're still friends and we do still see each other outside of school."

"Yeah. Look, I'm not mad at you; it's just not a great day today." She sat up a little straighter and tried to look interested. "So what are we working on?"

"Did you want to do peer-pressure? It was your idea."

"No. I don't know why I even said that. Let's do something else."

"I wouldn't mind working on drugs as an issue. You know how messed up my dad is."

"Yeah, that sounds good to me."

"Okay, I'll be right back." Brandon dodged back packs as he made his way to the front of the room. After a brief talk with the teacher he weaved his way back to his seat. "We got it first so we're all set. Do you want to work in the library?"

"Sure."

They worked on gathering resources until the bell signalled the end of class.

"I have a spare next," Brandon said.

Molly's eyes went wide for a second. "Oh, I forgot that. I have a spare too."

"I know. Did you want to keep working? I mean, we might as well get as much done as soon as possible. I know I'll have a ton of studying in a few weeks."

Molly shrugged. "Sure."

"Look at this; did you know there were medical applications for Meth?"

"Seriously? Let me see that." Molly leaned in closer to the computer they were sharing. "Treats ADHD? Well, that explains why ADHD is on the rise, kids just want drugs."

"This is going in the report."

Molly rolled her eyes. "I wonder which other drugs have legal uses. I mean besides weed."

"I can see it now. 'Hey Doc! I need another baggy of cocaine to treat my bad case of the flu!'" Brandon laughed.

"Right. 'Heroin is the only painkiller that works. Shoot me up!' Like that's ever going to happen."

"Medical junkies, the new epidemic that is sweeping our country, see the whole story tonight on your local news station – if the news anchor isn't high."

They were both laughing now.

"Look at these street names. Who thinks up this stuff? 'Horse', 'smack'?"

"Can you just see a drug dealer trying to talk to a farmer. 'Did you want to buy a horse? I've got a good one here from $1000.' 'How much horse do you got man?' 'One horse.' 'One gram or one pound?' 'No, he's about 400 pounds.'"

Molly was laughing so hard the librarian was glaring at her. "Oh, can you just see the look on the drug dealer's face! 400 pounds of heroin for a thousand dollars, what a steal."

"And then it's a real horse. He'd be pissed right off."

"Hi there."

Molly stopped laughing so suddenly she almost snorted. She and Brandon looked up to see Lance leaning on the study divider behind the monitor.

"Uh, hi Lance."

"Are you in class right now?"

"No, I have a spare."

"That's awesome. Can I borrow you for a little while? I wanted to talk to you."

While her heart pounded and she fought for enough air to answer Brandon jumped in. "She is working on a project for a class right now."

"But she's not actually in a class right now. So if she wants to take a break she can."

Molly could feel her face flushing. "He's right. I can take a break if I want to." She scooped up her bag and binder. "I'll be back."

As she followed Lance out of the library she fought the urge to look over her shoulder or turn around and apologize even though she knew Brandon was staring after her. Out in the hallway Lance just kept walking and Molly had to lengthen her stride to keep up. He wasn't looking at her and he didn't stop until they were standing out on the back parking lot.

"So … what's this about?" Molly asked, setting her bag down.

"I know this is really sudden since we only met last week and I've only really seen you twice but did you want to go out with me?"

Molly could only stare. To her credit her jaw didn't drop open but the words wouldn't form in her mind either.

"If you don't want to it's okay. We don't really know each other but we could take it slow, right?"

"No. I mean yes. I mean …" Her cheeks were getting hot. "I mean, no, that's not why I didn't answer right away. Yes, I'd like to go on a date."

"Not on a date. I meant dating, like going steady. Just you and me."

"Wow, yeah, okay."

"Great. Let me take you out for lunch today."

Molly nodded. "I have English right before lunch and then I can meet you …"

"No. I mean right now. We'll have a long lunch, somewhere nice. I have my car in the other lot."

She hesitated. *Brandon is waiting in the library, and I've never skipped a class before …*

"We'll have lots of time to talk. I want to know everything about you."

"Yes. Let's go."

She refused to feel guilty as he took her hand and led her to the student parking lot. His car was beat-up and old but at least he had a car. Molly knew there was no chance she'd get her own car until she could buy one herself, which would be after high school, and there was very little chance she'd get to use her step-dad's car for anything fun so any car was a great car as far as she was concerned.

He opened the door for her and smiled at her as she got in. As he started up the car he said, "What kind of music do you like?"

Molly was terrified of saying the wrong thing. She hadn't openly listened to her favourite bands since starting high school and she wasn't sure Lance would like what Kirsten and the girls made her listen to. "Oh and little bit of everything I guess. I'm not picky."

Lance smiled again. "This is my favorite band." The CD player had loops of wires poking out from behind it but it suited the car. The music that poured out of the speakers at a volume that prevented conversations in the car was a mess of drums and bass and screaming vocals.

It wasn't what Molly liked at all but she smiled and said, "They sound great."

He just nodded, put the car in gear, and pulled out.

Molly got off the bus after school feeling lighter than air. All she could think about was lunch with Lance. He had opened doors for her, held out her chair for her, complimented her hair and her eyes, and smiled that knee-melting smile the entire time. She had sat, enamoured, while he talked on and on about his family, his garage band, his gaming, his favourite music, his favourite movies, and whatever else crossed his mind. The constant attention kept the doubts at bay and when he kissed her before letting her out of the car at school she thought she'd faint! Her pocket chirped and she pulled out her phone.

"One new text message."

She didn't recognize the number but she opened it, curious. *"I miss you already,"* it read. She smiled at the screen, not realizing that she was standing in the middle of the yard while her mother waited on the step, her foot tapping in that way that meant trouble.

"Are you coming in or not?"

Molly's head snapped up and she jammed the phone back in her pocket. "Yeah, I'm coming. Sorry."

"Set your bag down and come sit in the kitchen. We need to talk."

Molly trailed after her mom, her cellphone practically burning a hole in her pocket.

"How was school today?"

"Fine. I'm working on a project with Brandon."

"And how was English class?"

Molly could tell she was busted and she knew better than to try a lie now. "I missed English today. It's okay though, I can get the notes from Julie tomorrow and I'll catch up the reading and questions. I'm doing well in English."

"Where were you?"

"I went out for a long lunch with a friend. It won't happen a lot."

"It won't happen again. School is very important. Look at your Uncle Chad! Without a grade 12 high school diploma you'll be stuck pumping gas or flipping burgers."

"What about Aunty Laurel? She's a university graduate and she's still working retail."

"Aunty Laurel has a degree in marketing and she only graduated two years ago. She's working retail to gain job experience so she can get a better job."

"Okay, fine. But it was one class! I've skipped one class in three years! You've pulled me out of more classes for appointments!!"

"I don't want to see you throw your education away!"

"You're making a big deal out of nothing, Mom! It was one class! I have homework." Molly stormed back to the front door and grabbed her bag.

Her mother followed after her. "Molly, I don't want this behaviour to spiral out of control. First you stay out late without asking for permission."

"I called!"

"You called after you changed your plans! Now you're skipping classes."

"Class, Mom, one class!" Molly pushed by and stormed down the hallway to her room. Halfway down the hallways she ran into Shannon.

"Molly, I got a part in the school play."

"Whatever. Get out of my way." She ignored the obvious hurt on Shannon's face and slammed her bedroom door.

She threw herself down on the bed and groaned into her blankets. The cellphone in her pocket buzzed again and she pulled it out as she rolled over.

"You're not ignoring me, are you Sweet <3?" the text read.

Molly smiled and hit reply. *"Sorry. Had to sit through a Mom lecture. I miss you too."*

She had enough time to pull out her binder and turn on her lap top before the phone buzzed again. *"What was your Mom mad about?"*

"Skipping class with you today," Molly sent back.

She pulled out her 'teens and drugs' assignment and pulled up the internet. Along with a search engine she opened Facebook. There was a friend request from Lance waiting for her. She smiled and clicked "Add Friend". His name popped up on her side bar the same time her phone buzzed.

"Does your mom hate me now?"

A second later Facebook chimed. Lance had started a conversation. *"Hey Good Looking, I was wondering when you'd show up."*

"Sorry, the bus is slow."

"You'll get your driver's licence soon, right?"

"Yeah, but no chance at getting a car." Molly bounced over to the search engine and typed in 'street names for drugs'. It wasn't exactly on topic but she and Brandon had found them so amusing she thought the rest of the class would too. *And a little humour never hurt.*

Facebook chimed but she ignored it and clicked on the first link. She wrote down the website and the list of street names for various drugs. Another chime but she hit the back button and went to the second link before flipping back to Facebook to read the back log of messages.

"Too bad about the car. So, does your mom hate me now?"

"Hey, are you still there?"

Molly rolled her eyes. *"I'm still here. I'm doing homework. And no, she doesn't hate you. I didn't even tell her about you."*

"Oh. Well that's for the best, probably. Don't tell her about me yet, she won't understand."

"You've got that right," Molly typed, rolling her eyes. Her mom was paranoid about all boys except Brandon just because she'd been eighteen when Molly was born.

"I like all your pictures you've posted. You're really pretty."

Molly smiled. *"Thanks. I haven't had time to go look at your profile yet."*

"I don't have a lot of pictures up. A bunch of my friends want to add you."

"All right," Molly typed. She took a deep breath and let it out slowly. She didn't have a lot of Facebook friends and she wasn't sure what other people would think of her favorite movies and music that she had listed on her page. In minutes she had fourteen friend requests, mostly from girls she'd never met but vaguely recalled seeing around the school. A few were from guys who she sort of recognized from the hockey and football teams or around the halls. Kirsten's brother was among the friend requests and that startled Molly. He'd always made it clear that she, and Julie and Amanda, were pains in his backside.

Molly clicked "Add Friend" as quickly as she could until all the friend requests were answered. She went back to the chat window. *"I'm going for a drink. Hold on."*

She stretched and took a deep breath. "This is crazy," she said to the empty room. "Why do they want to be friends with me?"

She peeked down the hallway making sure Shannon wasn't hovering nearby before hurrying to the kitchen. She knew she had hurt Shannon but she didn't want to deal with the apologizing and the long-winded "how I got the part" story that Shannon would want to tell. Molly grabbed a class of cola and hurried back to her room to find two dozen new notifications waiting for her.

*New comment on your picture.
*New comment on your picture.
*Four comments on your status update.
*New comment on your picture.
*New comment on your timeline photo.
*Five people like your profile picture.
*Eight people like your status update.
*New comment on your picture.
*Invitation to play Rainbow Slots.
*Invitation to play Zoo Ranch.
*New comments on your picture.

And on and on. Molly stared at the screen in shock as it chimed again and a new message from Lance popped up.

"I love your profile picture. You look so pretty. It's too bad you don't wear a lot of make-up. You'd be stunning with a little make-up on."

Molly smiled. *"My mom is a little old-fashioned when it comes to make-up. I'm not allowed anything fancier than tinted lip gloss and nail polish unless it's a special occasion."*

"You shouldn't let your mom tell you what you can wear like that. She doesn't want you to be pretty because she doesn't want you to be popular. She's just trying to control you."

"She's my mom; she's supposed to be in charge."

"Sure. But she can't run your life. She doesn't want you to be popular because you'll want to spend time with me and your friends instead of with her."

"My mom's not so bad."

"Would she let you date me?"

"No, of course not. She wouldn't trust you. She didn't like us hanging out together at the pool."

"There's your proof. She's already trying to control who you hang out with."

"Hold on, I need to respond to all these comments."

Molly took her time, bouncing between her homework and the comments Lance's friends were leaving on her profile and pictures. They were all being so nice, tell her she was pretty, that they liked her 'awesome' and 'kick-ass' hair-cut, that she had a nice smile, and that they were all so happy for her and Lance.

By the time her mom called for dinner she was glowing.

CHAPTER 4

Lance read the last text from Molly and smiled. One look at her at the pool and he'd known she'd be easy. That she was friends with Kirsten and he was buddies with Kirsten's brother made everything so much simpler. Now he knew for certain he'd made the right choice.

His phone rang and he answered with a cheerful, "Hey, what's up?"

"Just what is going on with Molly's Facebook page?"

"Kirsten, does your brother know you stole his cellphone?"

"Borrowed. And no, he doesn't. What are you doing?"

Lance leaned back and shook his head. "I'm building her up. You're her friend, Kirsten, you should be happy she's making new friends and meeting new people."

"But who are these people?"

"You're not her mother, Kirsten, so relax. They're friends of mine. My friends should have the chance to get to know my girlfriend, right? Or are you afraid that Molly won't want to hang out with you anymore? For a girl like Molly to abandon you that would probably hurt your popularity wouldn't it?"

"What are you playing at?!"

"Nothing, Kirsten. You worry too much, it's not attractive." He could hear her taking a deep breath, probably so she could screech again, so he said, "Give Trevor back his phone before he kicks your skinny ass," and hung up.

Kirsten heard the dial tone and swallowed what she had been about to scream. She hung up and left the phone on the computer desk where Trevor would find it. On her way out of the office she deliberately kicked over the wire garbage can spilling crumpled papers, junk food wrappers, and old tissues across the floor.

She went to her room and locked the door. She went back to her computer and started a conversation with Julie and Amanda.

"That bastard is going to ruin everything."

It took a moment for the girls to respond but when they did they're messages popped up simultaneously.

"*What's he doing?*" wrote Julie.

"*Which bastard?*" wrote Amanda.

"*Lance! And he's giving Molly more friends.*"

Julie typed back, "*Good riddance, let her go. I'm tired of her, she's needy.*"

"*Right, the needy fat girl is ditching us instead of us ditching her. How is that going to look?*"

"*Then let's just ditch her,*" Julie wrote.

Kirsten's first response was to agree, but then she backspaced and typed something else. "*Why? Why make this easy on Lance? Why not have a little fun with them both before cutting her loose?*"

"*What kind of fun?*" Amanda asked.

But Julie's response sealed the deal. "*I love it. Let's do this.*"

After dinner Molly tried to escape back to her room but her step-dad stopped her. "You mom and I are going out this evening. Shannon has agreed to do the tidying in the kitchen so we'd appreciate if you took care of the dishes."

"I have homework," Molly said, staring at the worn linoleum.

"I'm sure you're also chatting up a storm. You have time to put through a batch of dishes. You're old enough to be helping out. And taking a few responsibilities goes a long way to earning privileges."

"That sounds like a bribe."

"No, it's just a fact. When you act like a grown-up you get treated like a grown-up. We won't be out late and we expect the kitchen to be clean when we get back."

"Fine. I'm going to work on my homework."

She replied to all the new comments before opening her conversation with Lance. "*I'm back. My step-dad wants me to do the dishes.*"

"*But I'll miss you. I wish I could kiss you right now.*"

"*I can take my phone in the kitchen and we can talk. Or text.*"

"*Will you text me a photo so I can have you with me all the time?*"

"Yeah. I have lots of pictures on my phone."

"No. Take one special for me. Please."

"Sure, okay. I'll take it later."

"You know, you really have the potential to be gorgeous. I mean like show-stopping, every-guy-staring, amazing."

"You really think so?"

"I know so. And all my friends agree."

"Yeah, your friends are being really nice."

"Of course they are you're my girlfriend. That makes you popular now. And now that you're popular you should really think about how you look."

Molly's heart was suddenly pounding. *"Don't you like the way I look?"*

"Of course I do baby. I love everything about you. I just want everyone else to love you too. That's why I care about your make-up and your clothes and your weight. Because I care about you. Okay?"

"Okay."

A new conversation window popped up next to Lance's.

"Hey Molly. You didn't come back second period," Brandon typed.

"No, I went out for lunch instead."

"With Lance?"

"What do you want Brandon?"

"We are working on a project together, remember?"

"I remember. I'm working on it right now. I'm collecting more street names."

"Oh. Good."

"Look, I have dishes to do. Okay? Do you want me to send you any of the links I found?"

"No. I can get them from you in class tomorrow."

Molly closed the window and switched back to her conversation with Lance. *"I'm going to do dishes so I'm shutting this down. Text me?"*

"All night. Kisses!"

Kirsten's dad always dropped her off at school on the way to work. Amanda lived a block away and could get there as early as she decided to roll out of bed. Julie had her own car. It was easy to meet at school before the buses arrived.

"So, did you come up with a plan?" Julie said.

"Yeah," Kirsten said, flicking her hair over her shoulder. "Lance is building up her self-image, for whatever reason, so we're going to tear it down, without hurting her feelings of course."

"How are we supposed to do that?" Amanda whined.

"I'm going to try to talk her into purging," Kirsten said.

Julie glared. "You're supposed to stop that. How much skinnier do you plan to get?"

"As skinny as I can be. You don't see any fat movie stars or super models."

"There is that one star, she's huge!" Amanda said.

"Yeah, but all she does is comedy. She's fat and everyone laughs at her. If I'm going to be a star it'll be a REAL star. Besides, I don't want to act, I'd rather dance and you don't see fat back-up dancers."

"Fine," Julie huffed. "What about us? Because I'm not purging just to make Molly feel bad."

"Just change your habits for a little while. Don't buy fries or pop when Molly's around. Talk down about her eating choices. But we have to sound like it's for her health and appearance. Remember, we're the only ones who understand that she wants to be popular and we're just trying to help her."

Julie snickered. "I'm so in."

Amanda was pouting but she said, "Fine, I'll skip the fries."

That morning Lance was waiting for Molly by her locker when she arrived. He was talking to Kirsten but looked up and smiled as soon as she came around the corner. "Good morning."

"Morning," she said with a smile.

"Come here, I missed you."

She went to him and let him wrap his arms around her. Kirsten was smiling but it wasn't an 'aw that's so sweet' smile. Before Molly could consider what kind of smile it was Lance kissed her cheek. "I'll walk you to class," he said, taking her hand.

"Oh, I need my locker first. Hold on." She quickly untangled from his arms and swapped some of her books. "Okay, I'm ready. See you later Kirsten."

"Yup! You will!"

Lance kissed her cheek again at the door and she walked on air all the way to her seat in the back corner. As she sat down her phone buzzed in her pocket. She pulled it out and opened the text message.

"I'll see you at lunch sweet heart."

Molly smiled and texted a quick, *"I'm looking forward to it,"* before the teacher walked in.

After the national anthem and morning announcements they were sent off to work on their projects. Molly grabbed her stuff and followed Brandon to the library along with several other pairs of students.

They settled at a computer and Molly pulled out her papers. "See, I got a huge list of street names."

"I know that's what we were looking at yesterday but we need more than that for our project. See? I got some statistics on the number of teen over doses and how many teens are doing drugs, or at least the police estimate."

"But teens need to know what all the names for the drugs are so they can avoid them." She grinned at him. "I wasn't just taking the easy way out. I was doing something important too."

He grinned back. "Okay. You've got a point. Let's finish getting some statistics on drug usage and then we can outline the paper and the presentation."

Her pocket buzzed. "Okay, you get it all turned on. I'll just be a second."

"No cellphones in class, you know that. I don't want you kicked out. I need your help on this."

"Just for a second. The librarian isn't even looking."

Lance's message read, *"What are you working on?"*

"*Drug project. I have to work.*"

"*I miss you already. Are you working in the library with that loser?*"

"*I'm in the library, yes.*" She refused to call Brandon a loser but she couldn't stand up for him or Lance would be jealous and she didn't want that.

"*I'll meet you there and walk you to your next class.*"

"*Okay.*"

She set the phone down and smiled at Brandon. "All ready to work!"

"Good. You can't leave me to do all the work."

Molly rolled her eyes. "I know that."

After English class she met up with Kirsten and they hurried off to the bathroom. "I have a problem," Molly said.

Kirsten smiled. "Aww, trouble in paradise?"

"Not really. Look, you know how my mom is about make-up."

"Molly, I thought we went over this during the break. You were supposed to be paying attention."

"I was," Molly lied. "But I didn't get to wear any for the rest of the week and so I sort of forgot some of it. I don't want to look like a clown, okay?"

"Did you bring me something to work with?"

Molly opened her bag and waited while Kirsten rummaged through it, pulling out what she wanted to use.

Molly waited while Kirsten brushed and poked. Sometimes Kirsten would grab her by the chin and turn her face from side-to-side. Finally she said, "Okay, you can look now."

Molly hardly recognized herself in the mirror. Her eyes were huge and smoky. The eye shadow matched the blue in her hair. *I actually look sexy!*

"Here's some lipstick." Kirsten handed her a tube of maroon. "You really shouldn't buy pinks and pastels with your skin tone. You need richer colours. Really, you're so lucky that you're naturally tanned. Play that up."

"Uh, okay. Thanks." Molly put on the lipstick and handed it back to Kirsten. "Lance is probably waiting for me. Did you want to come and hang out with us?"

"I'll be there in a moment. I just have to make some room for lunch."

Molly's eyes narrowed. "What do you mean?"

"You should consider it, Molly. You could drop a few pounds without lifting a finger. Okay, you have to lift a finger, but that's only because it's the easiest way to trigger your gag reflex."

"Kirsten, are you throwing up on purpose?"

"Of course. That's what purging is, remember?"

Molly's eyes went wide. "Isn't that a bad thing? You should get help."

"You sound like my mom and she's a real drag. You're cooler than that. It's no big deal. I have it under control. I'll meet you down in the canteen. Okay?"

"Are you sure?"

"Of course I'm sure! Go on! I won't be five minutes."

Molly nodded. She paused at the door and looked over her shoulder. Kirsten was hovering by a stall. She waved Molly away so Molly shrugged and headed for the canteen.

Lance was leaning against a wall waiting for her. He smiled and held his arms out to her so she hugged him. "Wow, Molly, you look fantastic. I told you a little make-up would boost your looks. Now we just need to take you shopping for some really cool clothes."

"How do you know I don't have cool clothes in my closet?"

"I was just guessing based on what I've seen you wearing."

"What's wrong with my clothes?"

"Nothing. But it's like wine and beer. Beer is good, there's nothing wrong with beer, but wine is all around classier and sexier."

"So I look like a beer bottle?"

"Dark and curvy? Hell yes." He kissed her cheek. "But you can be so much more."

"Fine, I'll find something cooler to wear tomorrow, okay?"

"Okay. Why don't you make plans to hang out with your friends after school tomorrow?"

"I guess I could. I don't have any plans except a major homework assignment."

"You mean that project you're working on? Let that dweeb, Brandon, work on it for you. We have better things to do." He kissed her cheek again.

"Well, I'll have to wait for Kirsten; she's still in the bathroom. Did you know she's Bulimic?"

"Yeah. Has she talked you into trying it yet?"

"No. I can't stand throwing up. It's the worst feeling in the world."

"Well, you could always take laxatives, or just skip a few meals each week."

"Do you really think I need to lose weight?"

"No, you don't need to, but you'd look even prettier if you slimmed down a few pounds. How hard could it be to lose an inch or two? And you'd be so much sexier." He wrapped his arms around her. "No matter how good looking you are you can always be better."

"I'll think about it, okay?"

He kissed her cheek, dangerously close to her mouth. "That's my beautiful girl."

She wiggled free and settled on the floor. He sat beside her and wrapped an arm around her shoulders. From her bag she pulled a bottle of pop and a sandwich.

"You're eating lunch?"

"Yeah, I'm starving."

"I thought we just talked about this." He reached for her drink.

"I said I'd think about it. I'm really hungry."

He popped the drink and took a long sip. "Okay. But I really wish you'd think about your weight. Pop and bread aren't going to make you skinny."

Kirsten appeared at that moment with a bright smile pasted on her face. "She just won't listen to reason, will she?" Kirsten plopped down on the floor next to Lance and flicked a wave of blonde hair over her shoulder. Julie and Amanda walked over with their lunches on trays: salad and water for Julie, soup and water for Amanda.

"Ugh, you have pop?" Julie said. "That's so fattening."

Molly's brow furrowed for a second. She was certain, beyond a shadow of a doubt, that all three of her friends had been drinking pop at Kirsten's house. And she couldn't remember the last time Julie had ordered a salad from the canteen. She wasn't sure what to say so she opened her sandwich and took a big bite.

Fortunately the conversation moved away from the subject of her weight and dietary choices. Lance flashed a smile at the other girls. "We should all go hang out at the mall after school tomorrow."

"I'm in," Julie said. "My parents are working late. They won't care."

"I just aced a math test. My mom will say yes just because I almost never pass," Amanda said. She cracked open her water but didn't drink any.

"I'll need a ride," Kirsten said. "But I'm sure my dad will let me go."

"Molly?" Lance said. "You're coming too, right?"

"Yeah, of course I'm coming." Molly took a tiny bite of her sandwich. "It won't be a problem."

"But Mom," Molly wailed. "This is important!"

"How are you going to get to the mall? How are you going to get home? I need to go out for groceries tomorrow and Hank is working late. Luckily Barb is picking me up so I don't have to bus with all that food but someone has to stay home with Shannon."

"Mom, that's not fair!"

"Going to the mall is not important. You don't have any money to spend anyways!"

"Maybe that's because you never pay me for staying home with Shannon."

"You're not going tomorrow. Tell your friends you can go any other day this week, but not tomorrow. I'll even pay you for staying home with Shannon tomorrow so you can buy yourself something at the mall. Deal?"

"Fine." Molly stormed to her room and slammed the door. She went to turn on her computer to find it was only in sleep mode. The internet was open to a page on theatre productions. Molly snarled and yanked her door open. "Shannon's been in my room again!"

There was no answer so Molly slammed her door even harder.

Molly's friends had been really good about moving their shopping date. Only Lance had been upset.

"You can't let your mom run your life like this," he told her at lunch on Wednesday. "She doesn't understand you and she doesn't want you to be cool. I bet she's jealous of you because you're pretty and popular and she never was. Come on, let's go hang out outside last period today."

"I have a class last period. I only get one spare."

"Don't be lame, Molly. It's beautiful outside and it's going to rain tomorrow. Come on."

"Another day, I promise. I actually have a test today that I can't miss."

Lance sighed. "I'll miss you, but you're right. You go write your test and I'll walk you to the bus."

CHAPTER 5

Thursday morning Kirsten dragged Molly off to the bathroom and did her make-up before first period. "You need to go online and watch a few tutorials," Kirsten said as she fussed with the eye shadow. "This isn't hard to learn and I can't do this for you every day."

"I have been looking," Molly fibbed. It wasn't a full lie since she had searched make-up tutorial the night before. She had been too tied up talking to Lance to watch any of the videos but she'd tried. "I just had a fight with my mom this morning and didn't have time."

"What did you fight about today?"

Molly hesitated. "We fought over breakfast again."

"So eat the breakfast and purge. You'll lose weight and your mom will stop harassing you in the mornings. That's what I do."

"I'll think about it, okay?"

Kirsten stepped back. "There. Now you're gorgeous. No wonder Lance likes you."

After school Molly climbed into Lance's car and they drove to the mall with the windows all the way down and Lance's music blaring on the radio. He drove so fast the wind tossed her hair around and her heart was pounding at every corner.

The mall was buzzing with the after school crowd. Molly didn't often get to go to the mall, not with her step-dad working extra shifts and needing the car and her mom barely able to get enough hours to make ends meet. The twenty dollars in her pocket felt like a fortune even though she knew the others would consider it pocket change. Lance led them straight to the biggest clothing boutique in the mall.

"They should have something good here."

Molly looked around and forced a smile as her heart sank. There was no way she'd be able to afford more than a single piece of this clothing. She shopped at the big box stores where she could get cheaper versions of the same styles. Sure it looked cheaper too, but it was as close to 'cool' as she could afford.

"It's worth a look," she said.

Kirsten, Julie, and Amanda spread out across the store, fingering the fabric and holding things up against their bodies to get a better look at it. Molly trailed after Lance, her eyes lowered. When she did glance at the racks she saw right away that most of the styles weren't available in her size.

"Can we go somewhere else?" she asked softly.

"Don't you like the clothes here?" Lance asked. He pulled a shirt off the rack, studied it for a moment, then shook his head and put it back.

"Of course I like it; I just don't think we'll find anything for me."

Just then Julie came around a display with a black and silver shirt. "Try this one," she gushed and shoved the shirt into Molly's hands.

Lance nudged Molly towards the change room and smiled.

Alone in the change room Molly had a chance to breathe. She pulled her comfortable t-shirt over her head and pulled on the shirt Julie had picked out. It was snug across her chest in a way that made her feel self-conscious but it fit and covered her hips, which she liked. She turned towards the mirror and her eyes went wide.

The make-up combined with the new shirt and her own punk hairdo, the only 'cool' thing her mother had ever let her do, made her look so much older, and so much prettier than she was used to seeing. The shirt was slimming and sexy. Her eyes looked big and sexy.

This is what Lance sees. This is what my mom doesn't want me to be. This is what I could be. I have to have this shirt! Lance was right. He was right about everything.

A soft rapping on the change room door pulled Molly out of her reverie. "Is everything all right, Sweetheart?"

"Fine," Molly said as she scrambled to pull the shirt over her head and get it back on the hanger.

"Did it fit?" Lance asked. "I can ask Julie to find a different size."

"It fit," she called back, grabbing her own shirt.

"Did you like it?"

Her answer was muffled by the t-shirt she was pulling on.

"Babe?"

Molly opened the door. "I said I love it. And I love you."

Lance wrapped an arm around her shoulders and smiled. "I knew you'd like it. Did you want to try on something else?"

"No. I only have twenty dollars. Oh!" Her excitement flashed to disappointment.

"What's wrong?"

"I only have twenty dollars."

"So? The shirt is nineteen-ninety-nine."

"The taxes will be more than a penny, Lance." She sighed and started to hang it back up. "And I really liked it too."

"Then you'll buy it," he said, kissing her temple. "I'll cover the taxes for you."

As Molly accepted her bagged purchase from a smiling but bored looking cashier her friends came over.

"There's a sale on jeans I want to look at," Amanda said.

"It's not really a sale," argued Kirsten. "They give you a coupon for trying on jeans."

"So? I can use the coupon today, if I want to. That equals a sale."

Molly smiled. "I just spent all my money so …"

"You don't have to buy," Amanda insisted. "Just come try on some jeans and use your coupon next time you have money."

"I don't know if they …"

Lance hugged her closer. "If you don't want to go look at jeans we can always head back to my place and hang out – just us two."

His suggestive tone-of-voice sent a nervous shiver ran up her spine but she wasn't sure how to politely turn him down. Luckily her friends all jumped in.

"You can't ditch us!" Kirsten said. "We agreed to hang out at the mall together."

"Yeah, we're here to hang out with you," Julie agreed with a smile that almost reached her eyes.

Amanda was practically bouncing. "It's just trying on clothes, nothing more. It'll be fun!"

"If you're sure I don't have to buy ..." Molly pressed.

Amanda nodded. "Now come on!"

The store Amanda wanted was only a few doors down. The other girls flocked to the shelves but Molly held back, feigning interest in a sweater displayed near the door. Lance stayed close to her, as always, but she couldn't tell whether or not he was upset that she had chosen to stay at the mall.

Amanda bounded over and shoved a pair of jeans into her startled hands. "Try these on!" And then she was gone towards the back of the store.

Molly stared after Amanda for a moment and then held up the jeans. Lance turned and frowned.

"What's wrong?"

"I'll never fit these," she whispered.

"Do you want to ask the clerk if they have a bigger size?"

Molly shook her head, mortified at the idea of asking the size-zero clerk for something bigger than an eight. "I'll go look. If I don't find something then I'll ask." *Maybe*, she added silently.

Fortunately they did carry larger sizes. Molly selected the size she normally wore and, after a quick wave to Lance, went to try them on.

When they all wandered out Amanda had two new pairs of jeans and the others all had coupons for their next visit.

"How about supper?" asked Lance, steering Molly towards the food court.

"I should head for home. If you all want to stay longer I can catch a bus, it's no trouble." She tried to move away from the group but Lance held her close.

"I insist. Dinner will be my treat."

"That's sweet, but my mom ..."

"Molly, what do you want to do?" Lance interrupted, turning her to face him and holding both her hands firmly in his.

In that moment nothing existed except for Lance. Molly no longer noticed the angry stares from the people who had to dodge around them; she no longer cared that her friends were standing around waiting for her to make up her mind, or that her mom was waiting at home.

"Supper sounds wonderful."

They were lucky to find a table with four chairs, and an empty chair nearby that they could move over, but they knew it would be filled before they could place their orders. Lance smiled. "Why don't you wait here and hold the table, Molly? I'll surprise you with dinner."

Molly nodded. "Sure. I can call my mom while …"

He had her cellphone in his hand as soon as she pulled it from her purse. "Relax, okay? If you call your mom she'll just tell you to come home right away and we'll miss dinner together. She can't say no if you don't ask, right?"

"I guess so," she stuttered.

Her phone disappeared into his pocked. He dropped a kiss on her cheek. "I'll be back with the food."

Stunned silent Molly dropped into one of the chairs. Her friends followed Lance; only Amanda turned to smile at her. Molly forced herself to smile back while her thoughts and emotions reeled. A part of her wanted to be furious; she wanted to tell him off for stealing her phone. *But the he'll leave,* she thought, panic slowly overwhelming her anger. *He's looking out for me. He's doing this for me. He cares about me. I can't repay that with anger.*

By the time her friends returned she had talked herself around to being calm and grateful. Lance set a container and a fork in front of her. She stared at it for a long time, almost missing his apology.

"I'm sorry about your phone, Molly. Here. I shouldn't take your things. I just didn't want your evening to be ruined by your busy-body mother."

A salad, she thought. *Why would you buy me a salad? I hate salads.*

"Molly?"

"I don't like …" She made the mistake of looking up at him. His facial expression said concerned and curious but underneath that she sensed something else, something hard and cold. Everyone at the table was staring at her.

"What's wrong?" Lance asked.

"I don't like lying to my mom, that's all," she said, taking the phone back and dropping it into her purse.

"It's not lying, Molly. You're sixteen. You don't need a babysitter. We're not doing anything wrong. Just enjoy dinner. We'll get you home safe."

Molly opened her salad and hoped her sigh was soft enough to go unheard amidst the noise of the food court. She choked down as much of the salad as she could. It wasn't that she disliked vegetables but salads were her least favourite, even as a side dish, and eating nothing but lettuce was torture. She was so engrossed in her unsavoury ordeal that she didn't notice her friends smirking over their wraps. But Lance did and he made a mental note to find out what the girls were up to before they ruined his plans.

Molly waved to Julie as the car pulled away from the curb and sauntered up to the house, her new shirt tucked in the bottom of her school bag. Her mom was waiting in the living room when she came in.

"I thought you were going to be home for supper."

"We decided to eat out," Molly said with a shrug.

"You could have called. You have a cellphone."

"It slipped my mind. I have homework." Molly tried to leave but her mom wasn't finished.

"Molly, stop. This is about trust, and this is about me worrying about you. If you call and just say 'hey, we're eating out' then I know where you are and that you're safe."

"Last time I did that you yelled at me, remember?"

"Molly, every situation is different. Last time you said you'd be a few hours and changed your plans without telling me. This time you were already at the mall …"

"Last time I was already at Kirsten's."

"But I didn't know you were going to Kirsten's! I knew you were at the mall."

"Fine. Next time I'll call."

"That's what you said last time!"

"What do you want me to say? I'm sorry, okay. I forgot. It slipped my mind. It was noisy in the mall so I didn't even think of using my phone. I'll call next time. I …"

"You will keep your word and call next time or there will be consequences. Do you understand me?"

"Yeah," Molly muttered. "I understand."

Kirsten picked up the phone with a cheerful, "Hello!"

"What the hell are you playing at?" the voice on the other end snarled.

Kirsten frowned. "Who is this?"

"It's Lance! Who did you think it was? Santa Claus?"

"It's the wrong time of year for phone calls from Santa Claus," Kirsten said, her voice turning overly sweet. "But I couldn't be sure if it was you or a raging sociopath out for blood."

"It might turn out to be the same thing," Lance hissed.

Kirsten ignored his reply and said, "What can I do for you this evening?"

"What are you playing at?" he repeated.

"I'm quite sure I don't know what you're talking about." Kirsten flopped on her bed, unable to repress her smile.

"Why did you tell me Molly loved salads? Anyone looking at her at supper could see she hated it!"

"Oh, that! Well, we decided it was time Molly lost some weight. We didn't think you'd mind helping us with that. You care about her, don't you? I'm sure you want what's best for her."

"I want …"

"Yes?"

"Never mind that. You girls need to lay off."

"Give me one good reason why," Kirsten taunted.

"You're supposed to be her friends. Why are you making her life a living shit-hole?"

"Because she was never really our friend, we just let her hang out with us because we figured she'd take the blame for us, or entertain us, or something useful like that. And we were right. These last few days have been very entertaining." Admitting that after being adamant that she was Molly's friend was a risk but she was hoping he'd spill the beans if she did.

"Kirsten, you have the worst timing in the world," he growled.

"It's too bad I don't know what you're up to or I could help you with it. I'm very good at helping people."

"You'd like to know, wouldn't you? Just stay out of my way, okay? In a few weeks I'll be finished with Molly and you can belittle her to your heart's content."

Kirsten hung up on the dial-tone and sighed, all trace of her earlier smiles and teasing gone. "What does he mean, he'll be done with her?" she muttered. Just then her stomach cramped and she frowned. Her parents wouldn't be home until late so they wouldn't notice if she had nothing but a power bar for supper.

And they won't notice if you eat half a pizza by yourself and then throw it up before bed, she thought. The idea of pizza made her stomach relax enough that she could get out of bed.

"And maybe even a bottle of cola," she whispered, smiling again.

CHAPTER 6

Molly used to dread Mondays. The thought of everyone staring at her and judging her made her anxious and she felt like she was performing for Kirsten and the girls. Now she was tired of stepping around her family and listening to her mother's lectures. More than that, she missed Lance. Text messages and Facebook conversations weren't the same as seeing his smile and hearing his voice.

Lance was waiting by the lockers and he smiled at her. "Good morning, Beautiful. I don't know how but you get prettier every day. Come for a walk with me."

"I have class right away."

"You really have to stop arguing with me, Molly. Come on. Let's go for a walk, right now, before your friends show up and try to steal you from me. Your little dweeb friend will do your project for you."

Bewildered, Molly let Lance lead her away. Halfway down the hallway they crossed paths with Brandon.

"Hey Molly, you'll be late for class."

"I'm not going today," she said, holding her chin up high. Lance kept her moving away from Brandon.

Brandon frowned. "I'm not covering for you," he called after them.

"Pfft," Lance said, loud enough for Brandon to hear. "I told you he wasn't really your friend." Once they were out the front doors of the school Lance kissed her cheek. "Look at you go. You sure told him. I'm proud of you. You shouldn't let losers like Brandon control your life. If you want to go out for a walk with your boyfriend you should just do it."

Molly was shaking but she smiled anyways. "Yeah, let's go."

They didn't make it far. The principal, Mr. Penner, was just coming in from the staff lot with a briefcase tucked under his arm and a flustered look on his face. Whatever was bothering him didn't stop him from stopping them on the sidewalk.

"Lance, Molly, I'm surprised to see you two outside. You have a class this period, don't you Molly?"

Knowing that lying was pointless, Molly nodded.

"And I'm pretty sure you have one as well, Lance."

Lance grinned. "You caught us. We're sorry, the weather's just so nice and we hadn't seen each other all weekend. I bet you get a lot of kids playing hooky when the weather starts to warm up."

"We certainly do. Let's not add you two to the list. Back to class, both of you, before you get an absence and a call home."

"Sure thing," Lance said and turned around.

Molly, who was still tucked under Lance's arm, was forced to turn with him. She could feel her knees shaking with worry and embarrassment. But Lance stayed cool and relaxed, guiding her along under the principal's watchful eye. Inside they parted ways and Molly rushed to class, making it to her seat just as the teacher got to her name on the list.

"What happened to going for a walk?" Brandon hissed.

Molly glared at him. "I changed my mind. Why?"

Brandon shrugged and turned back around.

It was a note taking day and Molly found she couldn't focus. She'd be halfway done the points on the smart board when the teacher flipped to a fresh page. She didn't understand most of what she was writing down. And Brandon didn't turn around again the entire class which bothered her. He always turned around and whispered silly things to her.

On spare on Wednesday Molly and Lance wandered out to the school field. There was a soccer practice going on at one side and a lot of students headed home for lunch. Lance spread a sweater on the grass and they sat together, enjoying the sun and the unseasonal heat.

"How's Kirsten doing?" Lance asked. He had leaned back and wrapped one arm around her waist. His other hand rested on her leg.

"I think she's doing okay," Molly said. "She doesn't really talk about her problem."

"It's not a problem unless you lose control," Lance said. "You really should try it."

"I have to re-dye my hair soon," Molly said, changing the subject. "Should I do blue again or try something new?"

"I think the blue really suits you." He brushed a strand of hair away from her face kissed her deeply.

She revelled in the attention for a moment then pulled away. "There are people everywhere," she said.

"We're not having sex," Lance said. "Loosen up a little. We were just kissing."

"I know. I just don't like making a big show out of it. It's our relationship; they don't need to stare at us.

He smiled at her as he brushed his fingers over her upper arm and suggestively over her shoulder. His eyes moved from her face, down her body, and back again. "You're beautiful," he said. "If anyone's looking this way it's because they're jealous. You're mine, Molly and I love you so much."

She smiled at him. "That's really sweet Lance, I like you too."

His smile broadened. "At the mall you said you loved me."

"I know, I just … maybe we're moving too fast?"

He shook his head, his hand still running over her arm, almost brushing her breasts. The nearness made her excited and nervous and she had to take a deep breath to steady herself. "This isn't too fast. It's just a little fun."

"We are on school property," she said when he brushed his fingers over her stomach.

"Did you want to come to my house for lunch?" he asked, his hand caressing a little higher up her thigh than she was comfortable with.

"Kirsten and the girls are expecting us."

He shrugged. "It's just lunch, it's just once. I'd love to have some time alone with you." He kissed her ear, his tongue flicking against her skin. She tried not to shiver.

"They're my friends and I don't want to make them think I'm ditching them. We can do lunch at your house another day, when I can tell them what's going on, okay?"

Molly was shaking now. She didn't want Lance to break up with her but she didn't like his hand on her thigh like that.

And if he's like this with all these people around, what will happen when we're alone? I don't want to end up like my mom. And then he was kissing her and a new voice in her mind said, *He loves you, he's not going to do something to hurt you. Relax and enjoy yourself.*

It was first period after lunch and Molly was struggling through a math assignment. She glanced around but everyone else was working quietly. Molly looked at the page again; the only things that looked familiar were the numbers.

The intercom buzzed. "Mr. H? Is Molly in class?"

Everyone turned to look at Molly, except Mr. H. who was looking at the intercom. "She's here."

"Can you send her to the office please?"

Molly started packing as the teacher said, "She's on her way."

Someone nearby snickered but no one spoke as she hurried out of the classroom. Alone in the hallway she allowed herself to relax for a moment.

"I hate it when people stare at me," she muttered. She adjusted her bag and her purse and started walking towards the office. She grew tenser with every step, unsure of why she was being summoned.

The secretary smiled at her and asked her to have a seat on one of the chairs along the wall. So Molly sat and waited until her heart was pounding and worst-case-scenarios of expulsion were flitting through her mind.

The vice-principal's door opened and he waved her in. "Sorry to keep you waiting, Molly. I had a sudden phone call. Come in, please, I'll try to make this quick."

"I haven't been skipping class," Molly said as he closed the door behind her. "And I'm trying to catch up on the work I missed, really. In fact that's what I was doing when you called me down here. I really don't want to fall any further behind."

"I'm glad to hear that, but it's not your attendance I wanted to talk to you about today. It's your behaviour during your spares."

"I'm not hanging around by the lockers or eating in the hallways," she said, defensive. She could already feel her cheeks beginning to heat up.

"You're right, but I get the feeling you know what I'm talking about."

"I'm sure I don't," she said, trying to sound as confident as she imagined Lance being. She suddenly wished she wasn't facing this alone.

"Molly, this is a school, not a hotel, and not your house. We cannot allow public displays of intimacy on school property. "

"Public displays of intimacy?" she scoffed.

"You and your boyfriend cannot make-out on school property. That includes inside the school, and out on the soccer field. It also includes the parking lot and anywhere on the school grounds. Do you understand?"

"Yeah," she muttered, looking at her hands.

He sighed. "Molly, I understand that being a teenager is full of exploration. I was a teenager once, and not as long ago as most administrators. I know you feel the need to push at the boundaries and it's my job to keep those boundaries firm, for your safety and for the safety and security of the other students here. I appreciate you making the effort to attend class and catch up on your assignments so I'll skip the phone call to your mom, this time. But I don't want any reports of you making out on school property again. All right?"

"Yeah," she nodded. "Can I go?"

The bell rang and he nodded. "Yes, you may go. I don't want you to be late for your last class."

Molly sat in the bathroom with the egg timer and her thoughts, waiting for her hair dye to set. When she'd first cut and dyed her hair she'd told Brandon that she wanted to try every colour. Instead she had talked her mom into buying her more blue dye during their grocery shopping trip that afternoon.

That was a long time ago already, and Lance likes the blue, he said so.

Thinking of Lance made her head spin. Until she'd seen him at the pool she'd never even had a crush on a boy before, not even a celebrity. Then she had seen him at the pool, he had flirted with her and she had talked to him – she was sure her stuttered responses didn't count as flirting. They'd barely talked at Kirsten's but it was worth the lecture from her mom.

She'd barely had time to admit to herself that she did like Lance and then he was asking her out! Now he was walking her to class and the bus, holding her hand in the hallways, sitting with her at lunch, kissing her cheek and lips, and even choosing clothes for her when they went shopping.

He's making choices for you, said a voice in her head, the same voice that had advised against going to Lance's house the other day. The same voice she had been ignoring every time Lance suggested they do something fun together.

But this is what I wanted. Ever since meeting Kirsten all I ever wanted was to be popular like her. Lance is only telling me what clothes to wear and what bands to listen to because he knows what it takes to be popular and he wants me to be popular too.

But the voice didn't go away. *Is that all he wants?*

Molly frowned. *He loves me. He wants me to be happy.*

What do you want, Molly?

I want people to like me.

Do you like this new you?

Her only response was a shrug. The towel around her shoulders shifted and a thickly-wet strand of hair touched her neck, making her shiver.

The timer rang so she turned on the water and hopped into the shower, focusing on the heat and on washing all the dye from her hair.

When she was clean and towelled dry she wiped the steam from the mirror.

"I wanted to dye it green," she whispered.

Molly woke up to the sound of rain pelting her window. She was running late and threw on the first clean clothes she found before dragging a brush through her hair. She grabbed her bag and sweater and bolted for the front door.

"Honey, what about breakfast?" her mom called from the kitchen.

"No time, I'll miss the bus."

But there was time, because the bus was late. Molly waited fifteen minutes in the rain until she felt as grey inside as the clouds overhead. She got off the bus feeling hungry and cold and miserable. The warning bell sounded as she entered the school but the principal was standing there as she and the other bus students straggled in.

"I'll mark your bus late," Mr. Penner said. "Just get to class and there won't be any repercussions."

She tried to smile and kept walking. Her friends were already gone when she rounded the corner to her locker but Lance was waiting for her. For him her smile was real and she picked up her pace.

"You look like a drowned cat," he said, his smile both joking and sympathetic.

"Gee, thanks," she said, opening her locker.

He wrapped his arms around her even though her sweater and hair were still damp. "Aw, come on, it was just a joke."

"Sorry, it's been one of those mornings."

"Well, I have a surprise to make it up to you."

Her smile widened and she turned in his arms, all warnings of 'no public shows of intimacy' forgotten. "A surprise?"

"I mowed a few lawns," he said, smirking, "So I have some money to spend and I thought I'd spend it on you."

"That's sweet, but I have to get home to watch Shannon right after school. My mom has a meeting with a client and I can't be late."

"Then we'll go to the mall last period, just me and you. It'll be fun. And I'll have you home on time for your babysitting job. Deal?"

Molly thought back over the week since she'd been called to the office. Lance had been understanding and hadn't dragged her out of any of her classes, she had most of her assignments caught up even though she'd fail most of them, and her mom hadn't yelled at her in days. *I deserve a treat*, she thought. *Especially after such a horrible morning. It's just one class.*

"Deal. I'll meet you in the parking lot at last period."

He kissed her. "Great. I'll see you at lunch."

The rain let up long enough for Molly and Lance to get out to his car without getting wet but they had to run through the downpour to get into the mall. They tumbled through the doors, laughing like fools.

"I'm soaked again," Molly complained as water dripped from her hair and ran down her face.

"We'll stop at the washrooms and dry off, and then I'm taking you shopping. Come on, time's a-wasting!"

When she was damp instead of dripping Lance led her back to the jeans store and insisted she pick out a few shirts from the rack. With the coupon Molly had in her purse they got a great deal and quickly moved on. Lance's next stop was the drugstore where he directed her to the make-up aisle and helped her pick out some smoky colours for her eyes and a wine red lipstick.

"Bright red won't suit your skin tone," he said, matter-of-factly. "Trust me."

She nodded, feeling bewildered as he pulled her along with him.

The next store gave her pause. "You're not really going to take me in there, are you?"

"They're having a huge sale, now's the best time to shop here."

"But Lance, this is a lingerie shop! You can't come in here with me! I don't even think they carry my size here!"

"Okay. Here's some money. You go in by yourself; I'll just wait here on the bench. Tell the lady at the counter your bra size and she'll find you something that will fit you, I promise. I want you to have something that makes you feel sexy and confident."

"Lance, this is too much. You don't have to spend anything more on me."

"I want to. Molly, this is your chance. Just trust me and you'll be the most popular girl in school before the end of the school year. You'll be more popular than Kirsten and Julie and Amanda put together. Don't you want that?"

Molly nodded breathlessly. "Do you really think I can be that popular?"

"Of course. You're someone special, Molly. You're sexy and cool. You're fun and popular. You just need to make other people see that about you."

"But they won't see the underwear," she said, blushing.

"No. But you'll feel better wearing it. Just go try something on."

She nodded. "Okay. But if I don't like it I'm not buying it."

"See? Confident and cool. That's my Molly." He kissed her forehead and then settled on the bench.

Molly was openly surprised when the lady in the store showed her not one but an entire row of bras in her size. "I never came in here because I thought …"

The woman smiled. "The world's come a long way. Now even ample women are allowed to have nice clothes."

Molly took her selections to the change room and stripped to the waist. With her back to the mirror she put on the first one. It fit her better than anything she'd every bought at the big-box store and she liked the lace edging along the cup. She took a deep breath and turned.

For a moment she couldn't believe that the young woman in the mirror was her, but no underwear model she'd ever scene had a half-shaved head or blue hair. Her middle was still too soft but now she looked like she had real curves. Curious she put her shirt back on and stared at the mirror a little longer, liking what she saw.

When she finally rejoined Lance in the corridor she was flushed and she had a black bag hanging from her wrist. Lance smiled and pocketed the change.

"You look very, very, happy," he said, wrapping an arm around her shoulders. "Can I see what you bought?"

She held the bag away from him. "Lance!"

"I bought it; shouldn't I get to see it?"

"We should really get going," she said, starting towards the parking lot doors. "I have to get home on time."

He grinned and jogged a few steps to catch up with her. "Then you'll have to show me later."

"It's underwear, you' wouldn't be interested," she said, hoping he'd drop the subject. Suddenly the arm over her shoulder made her feel claustrophobic instead of comforted.

"I'm very interested in what you wear under your clothes," he replied in a smoothly seductive voice.

Her body reacted with a shiver that she couldn't control. Thankfully he stopped talking about it as they stepped back out into the slowing drizzle and made their way to the car.

They were halfway to her house when he said, "I can tell that I'm making you uncomfortable."

"I'm not uncomfortable," she lied, wanting desperately to be the cool, confident, popular girl he saw when he looked at her.

"You are, and it's kind of cute. I just want you to know that I wouldn't hurt you, Molly. We can get to know each other and have a little fun together, right?"

"I like fun," she said, hoping she sounded more confident than she felt.

"I know you do. Come to my house on Monday, after school. We'll hang out without the girls gawking at us and we can really get to know each other. Okay?"

"What do I tell my mom?"

"Tell her you're going to a friend's house after school. Maybe one of the girls will cover for you."

"Maybe. If my mom says I can be out Monday evening I'll come to your house. Okay?"

"You should just come over, Molly. Don't tell your mom, she'll only say no. She won't understand you. It's better if you just do what you want and forget about her."

"Maybe."

They pulled onto her street as the bus turned the corner out of sight. As soon as the car pulled up to the curb Molly grabbed her backpack and opened the door.

"Monday after school, don't forget!" he called after her.

She waved as she ran up the walk and he pulled away again. With her purchases already safely stashed in the bottom of her backpack she went inside.

"Who drove you home?" her mom said.

"A friend," Molly said, startled by the instant attack. Her mother tended to beat around the bush whenever there was a behaviour issue.

Joanna stood in the kitchen doorway, her arms crossed and her fingers drumming against her upper arm. "Which friend? I didn't recognize the car."

"Are you spying on me now?"

"No, I was waiting to see who you were skipping class with since the school called to tell me you had missed math class, again.

"I went to the mall, with friends, and I got a ride home. I didn't do anything wrong."

"Molly, this isn't about right and wrong. I thought we talked about trust already. I can't trust you when you don't keep your promises. And you skipped class again, so that was doing something wrong."

"Well, I haven't broken any promises," Molly huffed.

Joanna started ticking off points on her fingers. "You didn't call last week to tell me you'd be late coming home from the mall, you skipped Social Issues this week, you skipped Math this week …"

"But no more English classes. That's only one English class, one Social Issues class, and two Math classes and I haven't missed any tests!" Molly was grateful her mom didn't know about the talk she'd had with the VP the day before.

"We said no more classes, Molly. And now you skip a class again and come home with someone I haven't met yet. What's happening to you?"

"Nothing is happening to me."

"Who drove you home, Molly? It wasn't Brandon, it wasn't Kirsten or Julie. Did Amanda get her licence?"

Molly was tempted to lie but a quick phone call from her mother to Amanda's would get her in even more trouble. No matter how defiant she was feeling she really didn't want to bring the whole 'how could you lie to me' discussion into play. A safer lie was needed "No, Amanda didn't get her licence. We were with a larger group and I got a ride from someone who lived closer."

"Who, Molly?"

"Why do you care?" Molly said, getting louder.

"Because I'm your mother, I'm supposed to care who you're hanging around with."

"You mean you want to control who I spend time with."

"Molly …"

"You don't want me to have cool friends and I know you don't want me to have a boyfriend."

"Boyfriend? Is that what this is all about? Are you dating?"

"What does it matter? It's my life, my choice to make. You can't stop me."

"I'd still like to know what's going on in your life. You know I like to know the people you're spending time with, so I can reach them, or their parents, if something happens or I can't find you."

"I don't want you to find me! I don't want you controlling my life!"

"Is that what you think I'm doing? I think I've been very patient and understanding this past week. What has this new boyfriend been telling you?"

"My boyfriend cares about me. He understands me. He wants me to be popular and have lots of friends."

"He also wants you to skip classes and stay out late without calling your mother?"

"He wants me to have fun! You just want to lock me in the house until I'm old like you. You're afraid I'll repeat your life. You're jealous that I'm popular and you never were. You never could have been. And I have the chance to be popular. I AM popular. So leave me alone. I don't need you."

When she turned Shannon was hovering in the hallway. "Is everything okay?" she asked.

"Get the hell out of my way," Molly snarled and shoved Shannon aside. She refused to see how Shannon slammed into the wall and stared after her with tears in her eyes.

CHAPTER 7

Monday morning the office called Molly out of her first-period class. Molly packed her bag, glad to have a reason to miss the boring lecture on their final official unit. In the general office she was escorted straight through to where the vice-principal was waiting.

She slouched in the chair and let her eyes wander around the small room while the vice-principal opened a program on his computer.

"Molly, I'm surprised I had to call you down here."

"Why did you?" Molly asked. "I haven't been making out on school property."

"Your attendance has become a problem of late. You had near perfect attendance for almost three years, and then in the last week and a half you've missed at least two periods in every one of your classes. And the last time we spoke you sounded like you had it under control but then another truant showed up in the system on Friday. Can you explain that?"

Molly shrugged. "I haven't felt like going, I guess."

"May I ask what you're doing instead?"

"Just hanging out. School is boring; I just want to have some fun. I thought you were supposed to have fun when you're a kid." It was what Lance would have said so she repeated it to the VP, hoping she wasn't digging a deeper hole.

"Yes, that's a good point. But you aren't really a kid anymore. You're almost 18, Molly. You're old enough for a part-time job and if you missed shifts the way you're missing classes you'd get fired."

"So fire me then I wouldn't have to come back."

"You know school doesn't work that way." He sighed. "Molly, we're getting close to the end of the year. I don't want to have to kick you out of a class days before the exam. You have promising grades, don't let that slip away because your friends think hanging out in the middle of a field doing nothing is more important that an education."

"We're not standing around like a bunch of dorks doing nothing."

"I know that, Molly. But it doesn't matter what you're doing, the point is that you should be in class getting an education that will help you succeed in life."

"You sound like my mother."

"Your mother sounds like a smart woman. I hope you listen to her."

First my mother, now the VP, Lance is right, everyone is trying to control me. I've had enough of this. I'm not a child!

"My mother is a controlling bitch," Molly snapped, hoping to shock the vice-principal. "She doesn't want me to have any friends and you're just like her. I bet you were never popular either. You don't understand! My friends do understand and that's why I'd rather be with them than stuck in boring classes learning useless crap!"

"Molly, I suggest you watch your language. This meeting is just to inform you of where you stand."

"You mean threaten me into behaving?"

"I haven't uttered any threats but I will give you some hard facts. You need to smarten up and get your priorities straight, and fast. If you miss three periods in any one class you'll be kicked out. If you get kicked out for attendance you get an incomplete in the class and you have to do it over next year. The faster you complete your classes the faster you get out of this place and away from me. Sounds like a good deal to me."

"Maybe I don't want to be here in the first place," Molly muttered.

"Think about it. I don't want to call you down here again, Molly. You're not a bad student, and you're not a bad kid."

"Yeah, whatever." Molly grabbed her bag and stalked out. The period was only half over but she didn't go back to class. She pulled out her cellphone and sent Lance a text.

"Out early. Did you want to hang? I'm in the canteen."

Going to the canteen turned out to be a bad idea. It was only first period but the lunch ladies were busy cooking sausage and egg sandwiches for students with morning spares and an appetite for a big breakfast. The sausages smelled delicious and Molly's empty stomach was grumbling.

Just as she was about to give in and order herself some breakfast Lance came strolling in. "I only have a minute," he said, wrapping his arms around her. "Want to tell me why you're skipping class without me?"

She rolled her eyes. "I got called down to the office because I missed all of three classes."

"That just figures. Even the evil VP doesn't want you to be popular."

"Will you stay here with me? I have a spare next; we could ditch and go hang out."

"I'm in the middle of a test or I would skip with you. I'll see you as soon as I'm done. I promise I'll be out early too." He kissed her. "I'll see you in a little bit. And Molly, no snacking, we agreed that you'd watch your weight."

"Of course. I'm not even hungry. Go pass your test." She blew him a kiss and smiled until he was out of the room. She sighed and slumped against the wall. The smell of food was just too tempting and there was nothing else to do so she grabbed her bag and went to the library. Brandon wasn't there, he was back in class taking notes, but she turned on a computer and did twenty minutes of half-hearted work on her project anyways.

Her phone buzzed and she nearly dropped it on the floor in her rush to get it out of her pocket and read the text.

"I'm in the canteen. Where are you?"

"I just needed a walk to clear my head. I'll be right there."

She shoved her work back into her bag and logged off the computer. Brandon wandered in and smiled at her.

"Hey, I didn't think I'd see you again today. Are you ready to get some work done?"

"I'm just on my way to the canteen."

"You can't leave me with all the work, Molly."

"I worked on it today. Now I'm going for my spare."

"Class isn't over."

"Give me a break."

"Molly, is everything all right?"

"Yeah, why wouldn't it be?"

Brandon shrugged. "You've changed, that's all. I liked the fun, happy Molly."

"I am happy," she snapped. "You're just jealous that I have Lance."

"You can keep Lance, he's not my type."

"Well he is my type. Why can't you just be happy for me?"

Brandon's smile was small and sad. "I hope you're happy. Just don't abandon me with all this work, okay?"

"Fine. Split the project in two and give me a list of what you want me to do. I'm going now."

Molly tried to relax as she headed for the canteen but between her mom getting angry at her for skipping breakfast, the office getting angry with her for skipping classes, and Brandon angry with her just because she was finally happy, it was too much. By the time she got to the canteen she was seething.

"Whoa," Lance said as she dropped onto the bench next to him. "What's the matter?"

"Everything," she snarled and filled him in on her terrible morning.

He sighed and wrapped an arm around her shoulders. "It sounds like the whole world is against you, sweetheart. But that's why I'm here. I'll love you even if no one else does."

"Who doesn't love Molly?" Kirsten asked as she sauntered in, looking perfect, as usual. Even with the new clothes and the new make-up Molly knew she couldn't compare to Kirsten's pale-leggy-blonde look.

Lance thinks you can. Lance thinks you'll be even more popular than Kirsten. Lance has been right about everything else so far.

"My mom, the office, and Brandon," Molly muttered.

"Your mom doesn't want you to lose weight," Lance said. "But I think it's great you're trying to drop a few pounds."

"Oh, did you finally start purging," Kirsten said. "I haven't gone a pound over a hundred in two years."

"No," Molly said. "I skipped breakfast this morning and my mom threw a fit. It's not my fault she made a family sized pot of porridge without asking me if I wanted some first." She didn't mention the fight Friday afternoon since she'd already vented to Lance online over the weekend.

"You're right," Lance said. "She had no right to yell at you for something like that."

"And who cares about Brandon," Kirsten added. "He's a dweeb. He'll only hold you down in the end. He knows you're popular now and he's afraid of being left in the dust. Don't listen to him."

Lance smiled. "We understand you, Molly. We'll be your friends, your family, your everything. Don't let those other people get you down. I like it better when you smile."

Molly smiled and sighed. "You're right. You're always right. What would I do without you?"

"Let's hope we never find out."

Molly's bad mood only got worse over the day. Because of her skipped classes she was behind in every subject and every teacher handed her missed notes and assignments, and expected the work to be handed in before the end of the week.

At lunch she was ready to go buy food from the canteen but Kirsten started going on about the new season of clothes coming in soon and the big season change sale and how nice it would be if Molly could shop the boutique stores with them and Lance had jokingly pinched her thigh. So Molly had a bottle of water for lunch even though her stomach was starting to cramp.

She loaded her bag and stormed out to the bus only to be intercepted by Lance. He smiled, took her bag, and wrapped an arm around her shoulders.

"You're coming home with me, remember? I got us some beer."

"I want to Lance, I really don't want to deal with my mom right now, but I have a ton of homework."

"I'll help you with it," he said, steering her away from her bus and towards the student lot. "I already passed those classes. I might even have some of those assignments laying around in an old binder somewhere, and then you could just copy the answers. Wouldn't that be easier?"

"Yeah, it would be," Molly smiled, finally setting aside her misgivings and taking his hand.

She slipped into the car and they took off for Lance's house, driving right past the mall along the way. It was a nice house in a nicer suburb than Molly lived in. Looking at the neighbouring houses she didn't see any duplexes or townhouses which were the only types of housing on her street. Here the houses were mostly new with attached garages and big satellite dishes. Some of the houses were even nicer that where the girls lived.

"Your mom has a nice garden," Molly said.

Lance shrugged. "She likes digging out in the mud; I don't see the point in it."

"It makes the yard pretty, and it makes the house look like a nice, welcoming place."

He smiled and kissed her forehead. "You're such a sweetheart Molly."

They went in the side door. Up a step was the kitchen that was nearly twice the size of Molly's. Lance led the way down to the basement where a couple of couches took up most of the open space. There were doors along one wall and a small window near the ceiling of the other wall.

Lance went past the couches, turning on lights as he went. At the far end of the room was a bar fridge which Lance opened. He came back with two open beers. "Well, come on. Don't be shy. I basically have the basement to myself so we can just kick back and relax. No one will bother us."

Molly smiled and took the beer. She'd had wine a few times at special occasions and her mom had let her try beer once but she had found it too bitter and had never asked to try it again. Now she took a little sip and tried not to wince.

"Come on," Lance said again.

Molly joined him on the couch and looked around. It was a standard basement rec room but since her basement was mostly unfinished and used for storage she thought it was very nice, and a little intimidating.

You're popular now. You don't have to care if your mom has a horrible basement, she thought, trying to push the insecurities aside.

Lance wrapped an arm over her shoulder and pulled her closer. "I like spending this alone time with you," he said. "It's nice not having Kirsten or the others here chattering at us or watching us."

"I like Kirsten and the girls," Molly said.

"So do I, they're nice to hang out with, but not all the time. Sometimes I just want to be with you. And we should hang out with my friends some time too." He kissed her cheek then turned her face so he could kiss her lips.

The kiss was long and lingering and seemed to ask for more. It made Molly's stomach twist the same way waiting for a surprise did.

When he pulled away she leaned into him and kissed him again. He gave her kiss after delightful kiss all the while holding her close or caressing her arms and shoulders. It was the first time she'd really returned his affections and he seemed pleased so she continued.

He finally pulled away, smiling. "I'll put a movie on and we can enjoy our beer, and each other, for a few hours."

Molly tried to pay attention to the movie, even though it was some cop-comedy she had no interest in seeing, but Lance kept touching the back of her neck and her arms and legs. She kept shying away from his touch but he didn't take that as a signal to stop.

He got up, giving her a chance to relax a little but he returned shortly with another beer. "Oh," she said. "I'm not finished my first one."

"Well, drink up. I bought these for us."

Under his almost stern gaze she took three long sips of her beer. The amber liquid stung her throat and made her empty stomach do ugly flip-flops but Lance smiled at her and settled in beside her again.

By the time the movie ended she had reluctantly polished off both beers and was feeling light headed. As silence descended on the rec room Lance got up to turn off the entertainment system. The sudden absence of his body heat made her shiver.

The shiver made her giggle.

When Lance gave her a pointed stare she held her breath to stop the giggles. As soon as she let her breath out she started giggling again. "I'm sorry," she gasped between fits of giggles.

"What's so funny?"

"Nothing. I don't know." She tried to stop but the laughter snorted out her nose and set her off again.

Lance was smiling as he sat down beside her and she was too caught up trying to get control of herself to notice the calculating look under that smile. "Well, I'm happy that you're happy. I love a happy girl."

His deft fingers found her ribs and tickled her. It was a brief attack but it was enough to set her off again. He tickled her again, this time his hands found their way from her sides to her front and he ran his hands flat-palmed over her breasts. She giggled and swatted his hands away playfully.

The alcohol had released not only a torrent of easy-going laughter but a flood of hormones as well and Molly didn't feel any of her usual reservations at the physical attention he was paying her. They laughed and wrestled on the couch for a moment, stopping only when a half-full bottle of beer got tipped over.

Lance scooped it up before it could empty completely onto the carpet and took it, along with the empties, across the room to the sink.

"I love it when you're like this Molly."

"What? Drunk?" she asked as she got the giggling under tentative control.

"No, I meant happy and relaxed. You always tense up around me, like you don't trust me."

"I trust you," she said, her indignation making her pout.

He crossed the room with purposeful strides and kissed her hard. "Did you remember what we talked about? Did you do it?" he asked, breathless.

She nodded. She felt hot and flustered and couldn't tell if she was blushing. All weekend he had been asking about the new bras she had bought and he had convinced her to wear one today. Now determination and desire made his face more intense than she had ever seen it.

"Let me see," he said, his voice so gentle it surprised her. "I want to see how beautiful you are."

She nodded and lifted the front of her shirt, offering him the barest peek.

His tongue darted out, flicking over his lips and then gone again. "Will you take your shirt off for me?"

Under the buzz from the beers a voice in the back of her head was kicking up a ruckus but she couldn't hear it clearly so she ignored it and gave in to the attention he was paying her. The silver shirt slipped easily over her head revealing the lace-edged bra she had purchased Friday afternoon.

He kissed her and then stepped back, his phone coming out of his pocket. "You're just so goddamn beautiful, Molly. I want to remember you looking like this forever." He'd taken three pictures before she could even react to his phone being out.

"Oh! No pictures, please. That's not a good idea, is it?"

"It's just for me, Molly. It's just a little something to keep me company when I'm missing you."

She stood, intent on chasing him down, and he snapped another picture. This one was a little blurry but he kept hitting the button as she followed him. When she got too close he dropped the phone into his back pocket and wrapped his arms around her.

"I can't help it, Molly, you're too beautiful." He kissed her and let his hands caress her back where the warmth of his skin would relax her without panicking her.

When he pulled away she was breathing hard. He smiled down at her and said, "I'll grab us another beer, okay? You'll come and sit with me?"

She nodded and returned to the couch, retrieving her shirt along the way.

By the time he drove her home she'd had almost three full beers. She managed to make it up the path without tripping or veering off into the lawn which, in her beer-fogged mind, was a major accomplishment. She tried to be as quiet as possible, hoping to escape notice, but her mother was waiting in the living room with the lights on.

"You're home awfully late," her mother said.

"I went over to a friend's house."

"You didn't call."

Molly shrugged and leaned against the wall. "I forgot."

"I called Brandon, and Kirsten, neither of them knew where you were."

Molly frowned. "I thought I saw Kirsten in the parking lot when I left. She waved. I'm sure of it."

"Are you okay?" Her mom's anger had shifted to concern and she got up from the couch.

"I'm fine," Molly insisted, leaning back against the door. "I'm just surprised Kirsten didn't tell you where I was."

"You should have been the one to tell me! Molly, I was scared. I didn't know where you were or if I should be calling the cops! Where were you?"

"I was at a friend's house," she said again.

"Well then I need their name and phone number so I can track you down next time you go missing. And I'll need Julie and Amanda's numbers too."

"You're treating me like a baby!"

"You're acting like a baby."

Molly pushed away from the wall, closing the gap between herself and her mother. "You can't control my life! I'm allowed to go see my friends after school!"

"Molly, have you been drinking?"

"No."

"Don't lie to me. I can smell the beer on your breath. You're grounded for the rest of the week. I expect you home on the bus, every day. You'll be doing the supper dishes all week. And I'll be taking your cellphone."

"You can't do that!" Molly shrieked.

"You're lucky you need your laptop for homework or I'd take that away too. You broke the rules, Molly, you lied to me, and you're acting like an irresponsible child. So now you stay home where I know you're safe. If you can do the dishes and your homework all week then I'll give you your cellphone back after school on Friday and your punishment will be over."

"Take it!" Molly threw her cellphone on the couch and ran to her room in tears.

CHAPTER 8

Molly stared miserably at the test in front of her. She had missed most of the notes on this last unit and even though Brandon had photocopied his she hadn't studied. She filled in her best guest on the questions that sounded vaguely familiar and left the rest blank. She glanced around the classroom but everyone else was still scribbling away. Not wanting to be the first person to hand in her test she started doodling in the corner of the page. As soon as she saw someone else go up she grabbed her papers and handed them in.

"You can work in the library," the teacher said softly. "I'm sure your partner won't be far behind you."

Molly forced a smile, retrieved her bag, and fled.

The library was boring without her cellphone. She couldn't access her emails or her Facebook from the school computers and she didn't feel like working on Brandon's project. She pulled out a sheet of paper and started doodling again.

When Brandon came in he was smiling. "Hey, Molly, how's it going?"

"My life sucks," she muttered. "Can I borrow your phone?"

"Where's yours?"

"My mom took it."

Brandon frowned. "Why do you want mine?"

"So I can text Lance and tell him I'm out of class."

"But you aren't out of class. Molly, we have a project to work on. All the research is done but you need to start gathering the visuals for the presentation and writing your half of the script."

"Gee, thanks for planning my life for me."

"You asked me to, remember?"

Molly didn't but she wasn't about to tell Brandon that.

"Here's the list of topics you need to cover in the presentation and the research we gathered on it. And here's the list of visuals we need. I'll do my half of the speech and the written report."

"Fine. Can I at least do it later?"

Brandon sighed. "As long as it gets done. Don't leave me hanging, okay?"

"Whatever. I'm going to see if I can catch Lance's attention and get him out of class." She abandoned her scrap paper doodle and wandered out.

Lance was in the corner of the room that Molly couldn't see from the door and she couldn't risk being seen by his teacher. She gave up and made her way to the canteen.

A few minutes later Lance showed up. "One of my friends in the front row saw you hovering at the doorway. It took a few minutes for his text to get to me. Out early again?"

"I wrote a test today and didn't want to hang out in the library with Brandon."

Lance kissed her forehead. "Well, I can't stay. But I'll make it up to you later since we have the long lunch today. Okay?"

"That sounds perfect."

"Great. I'll see you later." He kissed her again and jogged off.

Wednesday morning Lance was waiting at Molly's locker with a metal water bottle. He smiled and handed it to her. "I brought you a present. I thought it would make you feel better after all the crap your mom is putting you through."

"What is it?" Molly asked, setting her bag down.

Lance lowered his voice. "It's beer. As long as you don't spill it or share it no one will know. You can drink it in class and make fools out of your teachers."

Molly smiled. "Sounds like fun."

Kirsten was smiling too. "You're so lucky, Molly. Lance is so good to you."

"I wish I had a boyfriend like Lance," Julie said. Her smile didn't reach her eyes and didn't last. "We have to get to class, Kirsten. You know we're practicing for the year end performance."

"Yeah, I'm coming. Save some for me, okay Molly? I'll see you at spare."

"I'll try!" Molly said with a wave. She smiled at Lance. "I really am lucky to have you."

He kissed her. "And I'm lucky I found you. I'll see you next period. Don't let that dweeb Brandon ruin your day."

"As if my week could get any worse. I'll see you later."

Molly took a long sip of the beer under Lance's watchful eye and smiled at him again. He waved and disappeared down the crowded hallway. She hadn't felt tense but that first sip of beer made her feel beautifully relaxed. She smiled all the way to her classroom.

Brandon had beaten her to class for perhaps the first time that year and he smiled at her. "You look like you're in a good mood today. Did you patch things up with your mom?"

"No." She dropped into her seat and took another long sip from the water bottle before tightening the cap and hiding it in her bag.

"Well, I'm glad you're happy today."

"Whatever."

"You know Molly, it wouldn't hurt you to be polite to people."

"Fine. I'm happy that you're happy that I'm happy."

Molly was halfway through her favourite song and chatting with Lance over Facebook when her mom called for her. She took her time pausing everything and stuck her head out her bedroom door. "What is it?" she yelled.

"Company! Why don't you come and sit for a while?"

Molly huffed. "Fine!" She came into the living room and her frown deepened. Brandon and his mom were sitting on the couch.

"Hey, there you are. Grab a chair from the kitchen and join us. You've been cooped up in your room for days."

"I have a lot of homework," Molly muttered as she fetched the chair.

Barb smiled. "Brandon's told me all about the project you two are working on. Maybe when it comes time to practice your presentation you'll let us watch."

"I'd like that," Joanna said.

Brandon forced a smile. "We could try to arrange that, I guess."

"Sure," Molly said. "Why not? Doing it once in front of people is bad enough, what's two or hell, even three more times?"

"Molly," her mom snapped. "Language."

"Whatever."

Her mom frowned and an awkward silence hung in the air.

"I'm sure you two have a lot of work to do," Joanna said. "I know Brandon didn't bring his bag but they can work in Molly's room for a little while."

"Mom, stop letting people into my room!"

"A girl's room is her private place," Barb said. "And she wasn't expecting us. I'm sure there're undies everywhere."

"Fine," Joanna. "At least grab your laptop and go downstairs."

"I'll meet you down there," Brandon said.

Molly slunk back to her room. She reopened the conversation with Lance. *"Brandon is here."*

"Did you invite him?"

"No. His mom and my mom are friends. She's here for a visit and he tagged along. My mom's making us do homework."

"So you'll be gone?"

"For a little while. I have to take my laptop downstairs and share."

"I'm sorry sweetheart. I'll miss you. Message me when you're alone again."

"I'll miss you too."

Molly closed the laptop and dragged it down the stairs. Brandon had cleared the coffee table and dragged it closer to the one love seat that had been abandoned down there.

"How far have you gotten?" he asked her.

"I read all the research," Molly lied. "What about you?"

"I'm about a third of the way through the written report. I wish you'd use the class time to work, I'm really worried that we'll fail this project."

"Relax. I have everything under control."

"Will you have the visuals done by Monday?"

"Sure."

"What sorts of images did you have in mind?"

Molly opened the laptop. "Pictures of the different drugs, I guess, like a bag of cocaine. Some graphs. Teachers like graphs. Maybe stats on teen deaths, if I can find one."

"There was one in the research I gave you."

"Right. That's why I thought of including it. I just forgot."

"Did you really read the research?"

"Of course I did." She logged in and started up the internet. "What should I search for?"

"Didn't I interrupt you? Weren't you already working on it?"

"Sure, but I wasn't sure if you were going to sit and watch me do my own thing or if we were going to work together."

"You do your own thing. It's my turn to sit back and do nothing."

"Do you see what I mean now?" Joanna said as soon as the teenagers were down the stairs. "I just don't know what to do, Barb. It's like she's become a stranger these last few weeks."

"We went through it too," Barb replied. "I went a week without talking to my mom once. When I call her too often she likes to remind me of that little fact – followed by the suggestion that I repeat it."

"Your mom has an evil sense of humour."

"Yeah. Look, Molly's going through a phase. You said there was a boy involved? She'll get her heart broken and she'll come crying to you and apologizing. Just remember to forgive and forget when the time comes."

"I never know what to do with her. My parents were so strict, so conservative, that I rebelled as hard as I could and ended up out on my ass with a baby. But your parents were so laid back that you wound up pregnant too. I'm trying to let her grow up but I'm terrified of letting go and now, the way she's yelling all the time, I'm terrified that I'm smothering her afterall."

Barb smiled. "They're all different, and walking a middle ground is hard. You two will get through this. Just watch. I give it until the end of summer."

After supper Molly tried to escape to her room but her mom called after her, "Molly, I want to talk to you. Come sit with me in the living room."

Molly heaved a sigh. "Fine." She dropped onto the couch and crossed her arms.

Her mom took a deep breath and let it out slowly. "I'm worried about you, Molly. You're not acting like you anymore."

"Of course I'm acting like me."

"The Molly I know and love isn't rude to her friends."

Molly rolled her eyes. "Barb is your friend, not mine. And Brandon and I aren't friends anymore, we're just stuck working together."

"When did this happen? Why did it happen? Did you two have a fight?"

"Brandon's a dweeb, he's a loser."

"Molly!" her mom gasped.

"What? I have other friends now. Popular friends. And they all think I'm cool and pretty. I'm happy so you should be happy for me."

"I am happy that you have friends but I worry that they're not the right friends."

"What would you know about it?"

"I was a teenager too, Molly. One of my best friends ditched me for the chance to be popular. Her popularity didn't last and by then I had moved on with other people. We were too different after everything that had happened to be friends anymore."

"I don't want to be friends with Brandon so why do I care?" Molly huffed and rolled her eyes.

"Where is all this attitude coming from?"

"What attitude? I' just tired of you interfering in my life."

"I'm not interfering, I'm parenting. I'm supposed to know where you are and who you're with. I'm supposed to set the rules and boundaries that keep you safe."

"I don't need you anymore. I don't want you in my life anymore. Just butt out and leave me alone."

"You're walking a dangerous line, Molly Anne."

"You're not going to intimidate me," Molly snapped back. "You don't care about me. You don't want me to have friends. You don't want me to date. You're not setting boundaries you're building a fucking cage."

"Molly!"

"I'm tired of living in your little cage! I'm tired of being who you want me to be. I want to grow up and be me. I want to be popular and cool. I want a boyfriend. I want to drink. I'm doing what I want for a change and you're not stopping me anymore."

Her step-dad appeared in the kitchen doorway. "I think everyone needs to cool down," he said. He sounded calm and reasonable.

Molly didn't want calm and reasonable. "No one asked you!" she snapped. "You're not my dad so this is none of your business."

"No," he said, still keeping his voice calm. "I'm not your biological dad I'm just your step-dad. But I care about you and your mother …"

"Well I don't care about you."

Hank frowned.

Molly pushed on. "I never needed you. I was just fine before you showed up! You showed up and took my mom away from me and now you're upset that I want her to butt her nose in my business. I hate you and I hate Shannon too!"

"You hate me?" asked a very small voice from the hallway.

Molly turned on her younger sister. "You're small and annoying. You're always touching my things and going in my room. You're noisy and I hate you! I hate all of you."

Tears welled up in Shannon's eyes and she screamed "Well I hate you too! You're the worst big sister ever!" She turned and fled, sobbing. Her dad followed after her, his face serious.

Molly turned back to her mom, anger overwhelming all other emotions. "Just leave me alone from now on!" She stomped down the hall to her room and opened her computer.

At least online there are people who understand me and care about me. I hate being trapped here.

But online wasn't the support network she was hoping for. No one was online and waiting to chat, not even Lance, so she poured her anger out in a long-winded post that ended with "I hate my family".

When the dishes were washed, and dried, and put away, and the counters and table wiped and dried, and the floor swept, Hank sighed and made his way down the stairs to the little room his wife used as an office.

The second hand couches sat in the middle of the unfinished rec room on a thin area rug in tacky, outdated colours. It had never bothered Hank before; the house had always been a bit of a work in progress. *And didn't we just get Molly's laptop and those new couches for the living room? It's not like we're living in the Stone Age.* But today the second hand furnishings and unfinished room made him feel like somewhere along the way he had failed at the one job that really mattered, the job of taking care of his family.

And they are my family, no matter what Molly thinks or says, he thought with fierce pride.

Molly had been six when Hank had met Joanna. Her car had broken down in a parking lot on one of those plus forty days that still made him thankful she'd left Molly with Barb that day. Dozens of people walked right past her as she stared hopelessly at the engine of her car and he couldn't understand why. Maybe her clothes had been a little too well-worn, maybe the car had been a bucket of rust, but Hank had taken one look at Joanna and had seen strength in her tired eyes. *Or maybe I noticed the strength when she swore like a sailor and kicked the tire*, he thought, amused at the memory.

They had become tentative friends. A woman so badly rejected with a child to care for didn't open her heart easily; he understood and accepted that, just as he accepted her fierce pride and deeply hidden fragility. And when they had started seeing each other romantically it had taken Molly even longer to warm up to him than it had taken Joanna. By the time Shannon was born, two years later Molly had mostly accepted him as a friend, if not as a parent and in the years since he'd thought they had gotten closer, or at least come to a comfortable understanding with each other.

Taking a deep breath he knocked on the door which was rarely closed unless Joanna was in the middle of a conference call. It really was too late in the evening for her to be on the phone – unless she was calling Barb, but he didn't hear any voices so he stepped inside.

The computer was on and an image was open in some graphic design program that Hank barely understood and certainly didn't know how to use. Some days he envied her creativity. Today he was more concerned about the way she sat staring blankly at the screen.

He put his hands on her shoulders, squeezing gently – her shoulders were locked with tension. "How are you feeling?" he said.

Her shoulders rose and fell.

"She doesn't mean any of it," Hank said, hoping he wasn't giving voice to a lie.

"What if she does?" Her voice shook. "What if she doesn't need me anymore? What if she doesn't love me anymore?"

"Did you need your mom at sixteen?"

Joanna opened her mouth to answer then closed it and paused to think. "I thought I didn't," she said at last. "And maybe I didn't need my super conservative mom but I needed *a* mom."

"She still needs you, but maybe you need to be there from the background for a while so she can figure some things out for herself. As for loving you, well, if you could love your mother even after she kicked you out I'm sure Molly will come to realize that she does love you and that this is just a passing anger."

"I tried," Joanna said her voice dropping to a near whisper. "I didn't want to be my mom so I tried to give her space to grow, space to be herself. Where did I go wrong?"

"I don't think you did. I think this is about Molly and her friends and this new boy she's seeing. I think Barb's right. In time Molly's going to get her heart broken and she's going to come back to us in tears. We just have to be ready to love her when that happens."

"What if ..." It was a question she couldn't ask, a question she didn't want to think needed to be asked. She reached up and gripped Hank's hand.

"We won't kick her out," Hank replied. "And you're working from home so you can help her. She'll be able to finish school and our family will be a little bigger." He leaned down and kissed her cheek. "You did everything you could to prepare her, Joanna. She'll make her own choices, and some of them will be pretty dumb, if I remember being a teenager. But she'll live."

"I hope you're right."

"Does this need to be saved?" He gestured at the monitor.

"No. I didn't touch it."

"Good." He powered the computer off and helped her out of the chair. "Let's get some sleep."

CHAPTER 9

Lance was waiting in the library when Molly and Brandon came in to work on their project. He smiled and wrapped his arms around Molly. "I saw your post yesterday. Are you okay?"

She shrugged. "I guess so."

"I told you this might happen when you tried to be popular. I'm sorry your mom couldn't be cool with everything."

Brandon scowled. "We have work to do so could you get lost? You're a serious distraction."

Lance stared at Brandon for a long moment and Molly could feel her heart thundering in her chest.

What do I do? What do I do?

Finally she snickered and rolled her eyes. "Yeah, right, nice one Brandon," she said and smiled at Lance. "I don't want you to leave."

"The project …"

"We're working on separate pieces now, right? So you work at that computer on your piece and we'll go work over on that computer where we won't distract you. Okay?"

Lance was grinning. "Come on, Molly. Let's not distract the loser any longer."

They wandered off down the row of computers, holding hands and snickering to each other.

Brandon opened the report he had been working on and tried to focus on it. Every time Molly giggled he would look up and glance down the aisle at her. Lance was sitting very close to her and talking in a hushed voice, his lips right against Molly's ear. Brandon frowned and kept working, trying to ignore them.

Unable to focus any longer he opened a new document and began to type everything he had witnessed in the last week or so.

Julie doesn't like Molly, I've seen her sneer and snigger at Molly when Molly isn't looking. Why did they let Molly into the group this fall?

Kirsten is up to something. She's heading off any fights between Julie and Molly, but why? Does she really care about keeping Molly in their group?

She's skipping meals (Molly's mom told my mom the other day). Is she becoming anorexic? Is Lance doing that to her? Or is it the girls?

She's obsessed with Lance and she's making bad choices because of it.

She's cutting classes and shirking her homework. She's never done either before.

She's using words like loser and dweeb. I've never heard her insult anyone before.

Molly is dressing differently. She's wearing make-up.

She doesn't want to talk to me at all. Before Spring Break she would talk to me as long as the girls weren't around.

This isn't about me, I can't make it about me, but she's hurting me and we used to say we'd always be friends. I could handle drifting apart but I hate how she's treating me. But what can I do about it?

Why is she changing? What else is changing? What else is Lance coercing her into? Who else is she pushing away? Does she really want popularity this badly? She's always talked about being popular, like Kirsten and her friends, but now it's an obsession.

Does Lance really love her? Does he care about her? If not, then what is he after? Why Molly? I know she's wonderful and fun but does Lance see that?

He sighed and closed the list without saving.

Molly wants me out of her life and after everything she's said I should just go. But I don't trust Lance and I don't trust Molly's so-called friends. There's nothing I can do but wait and hope that this isn't what it seems.

Friday afternoon Molly and Lance came out of the school building hand-in-hand. He started walking towards the student lot, pulling her with him. She tugged back.

"I'm still grounded, remember?"

Lance sighed. "I'll give you a lift home, right now. I promise, no side trips, no errands. I just want to spend a little more time with you. Come on. Your mom wants you home right after school, right? I can get you there faster than the bus. In fact we can stop and have a little drink before we leave the lot. Come on."

Molly smiled. "Okay. But you have to get me home before the bus."

They climbed into Lance's car and he handed her a metal water bottle. "Here's the beer. Enjoy."

Molly still didn't like the taste but she took the bottle and drank. He smiled and put the car in gear. "Let's get you home."

Lance had to stop for gas but they still pulled up in front of Molly's house just as the bus rambled down the block ahead of them. Lance leaned over and kissed her. "I'll see you this weekend."

"I can't wait."

Molly jogged up to the house. "I'm home!"

Her mom was in the kitchen cutting vegetables. "I heard the bus go by and I thought you'd decided to skip out on me again."

"Of course not. I just took my time coming in. It's really nice outside. I might take my laptop into the back yard to work this afternoon."

"Well, as promised, here's your cellphone." The phone was resting on the table.

Molly crossed the room and picked it up.

"Molly, I've been getting some distressing calls from the school. You're very close to being kicked out of your classes." Joanna set the knife down and turned.

"I'm doing fine! I'll have all the assignments caught up and handed in on Monday."

"Do I smell alcohol on your breath again?"

"No."

"Molly, you'd better not be drinking at school! Don't you understand how important school is?"

"Everything is fine. Lay off already."

"Everything is not fine."

"Are you going to ground me again?"

"I'll un-ground you after dishes tonight."

"That wasn't the original deal!!" Molly wailed.

"I should have made it clear that you needed to earn your freedom."

"I did earn it! I was home right after school every day this week."

"And today you came home drunk."

"I am not drunk. Watch. Z. Y. X."

"Oh stop it Molly. Who's giving you the alcohol?"

"It was less than one beer! I'm not drunk and I wasn't drinking during school hours."

"You're underage! You can get in serious trouble for this."

"You just want to stop me from having fun. You yell at me and ground me and tell me it's for my own good but it's all for you. You don't want me to be popular. You don't want me to have a boyfriend. You don't want me to have any friends at all! You won't be happy until everyone at school thinks I'm a loser!"

"Molly that's not true."

"Bullshit!"

"What your language!"

"Make me."

"You're not leaving the house this weekend. Maybe that will clear your head."

"I HATE YOU!"

The anger disappeared from her mom's face. "I hope you don't mean that."

"Or what? You'll ground me until I come grovelling and apologizing? I hate you. I hate all of you. I don't need you anymore!" Molly ran to her room and slammed the door as hard as she could. She collapsed on the bed and started sobbing.

Molly ate her supper and did the dishes in sullen silence. She returned to the safe haven of her room where her friends were waiting. She had posted about her fight with her mom and comments of support and understanding had been pouring in all afternoon.

"At least she didn't take my phone and computer," Molly muttered.

As if on cue her cellphone rang. She answered right away hoping her mother hadn't heard it.

"Hello?"

"Hey sweetheart. I'm sorry I got you in trouble."

"Who cares? I hate her. You were right, she doesn't understand me."

"Are you okay?"

"Of course I'm okay. I'm stuck at home all weekend though."

"Damn. I'm going to miss you. Isn't there some way we can see each other?"

"Not unless you plan on coming over and introducing yourself to my mother. And she probably hates you more than she hates me right now."

"She doesn't have to know."

Molly rolled her eyes. "And how am I supposed to sneak you in here?"

"Why don't I sneak you out?"

Molly laughed.

"No, I'm serious. I'll come by about ten pm. It's mostly dark by then."

A nervous shudder when through her as she realized he really was serious. She took a deep breath and made her choice. "You'll have to come later. My step-dad is working a double and won't be home until midnight. My mom always waits up for him."

"Fine. Twelve-thirty then. I'll park in the back lane and text you when I get here. Just turn in around eleven, make a big show of getting a drink and yawning, you know, then crawl under the covers in your clothes and wait for me. Just remember to bring your backpack with you, okay?"

"Okay," Molly said, feeling a thrill of excitement.

"I love you Molly."

"I love you too."

Her phone was on silent so the only indication that she had a text was the screen lighting up. She hit 'read' on the screen and the message came up.

"*I'm here.*"

"*I'm coming,*" she texted back.

Carefully she slipped out of bed and opened her bedroom door. The lights were all out, a sure sign her mom had turned in for the night. Molly tried to keep her steps light as she made her way past the other bedrooms. The hardest part was the side door. She had to unlock it, open it, open the screen door, close the main door, lock it again, and close the screen, all without alerting her family.

She held her breath through the whole thing. But then she was on the back stoop with the house locked up and not a sound from inside. She let out a sigh of relief and bolted through the yard to the back gate.

Lance's car was parked right outside the yard in the back lane, just as he had promised. Molly climbed in and giggled. "I thought I was going to get caught," she said.

"You're with me now. Let's go have some fun."

They pulled away from the house and into the night.

CHAPTER 10

They started the evening with a beer and some music in Lance's basement. As the CD ended Lance took the empty bottles and stashed them in the box beside the fridge. When he came back he wrapped an arm around her. "I'm so glad you're here," he said.

He started kissing her cheek and lips and even down her neck a little. She melted at the attention and smiled. The hand on her thigh squeezed gently. He took her hands in his and moved them so she was hugging him.

The kisses were teasing and light and made her heart race, especially when he lightly flicked the tip of his tongue over her lower lip. She squeezed his shoulders as he ran his hands down her arms and sides. His hand moved over her breast and caressed it gently but firmly through her shirt.

"No, please stop," Molly said, pulling away.

"You're my girlfriend. Come on, don't be such a drag." He wrapped an arm around her and pulled until she leaned against him.

"You'll stop?"

"I promised I'd never hurt you, didn't I?" He tucked a finger under her chin and tilted her face up until he could kiss her. His kisses were gentle at first and she relaxed. He used the kisses to draw her into the moment, to distract as well as seduce.

His hands caressed her shoulders, casual and firm, like a massage that only hinted at the erotic. He rubbed her arm, all the while letting his kisses build heat between them.

She turned into him, her fingers tentatively brushing his cheek. When he flicked a tongue over her lips she gripped his arms, pressing herself against his chest.

He brushed her ribs and stomach through her shirt and she trembled in his arms. His hand slipped under the hem of her new shirt with expert deftness and closed over her breast.

She jerked back and slapped his hand away. "I said no. I don't want to go that far."

"What the hell, Molly, it's a little harmless touching. Come here." He reached for her to draw her close again.

"I don't feel like it anymore. Let's put on some music or a movie or something." Her stomach rumbled audibly and she giggled. "I'm starving. I skipped lunch and supper. I could really use something to eat."

"Let me get you another beer."

"I probably shouldn't."

"I thought you were cool but you're really just a loser, aren't you?"

Molly sat in stunned silence as Lance went to the fridge and pulled out two more beers. He came back and handed one to Molly.

"Don't be a buzz kill, Molly. Drink the beer."

Shock was threatening to give way to tears so she drank some beer. It was bitter and made her throat tighten but she didn't complain.

He took a deep breath and his shoulders relaxed. He stared straight ahead, the bottle tucked between his knees, both hands on the neck. "I'm sorry, Molly. I love you so much and then you do something frigid and I'm scared you don't love me as much as I love you."

"I do love you."

"Then come over here and show me." He set his beer down and tried to draw her close again.

"I do love you Lance."

"Show me." He moved quicker this time, his kisses were more demanding and his hands more forceful. He leaned her back so her beer almost spilled. His hand when straight under her shirt and groped her breast. Where they should have been pleasure and desire Molly felt only terror rising inside her. She dropped her beer. The bottle bounced harmlessly on the carpet and the amber liquid glugged out.

She pushed against his chest and struggled beneath him. He was too strong, too heavy, and too set on taking what he wanted to be shoved aside.

She opened her mouth to scream and he pushed his tongue between her lips. Desperate now she bit his tongue.

He jerked back and slapped her.

"You fucking little cock tease. Who the hell do you think you are anyway? You walk around dressed like a whore and you get mad when I want to touch you? I've been buying you lunch and liquor and this is how you repay me? I expected you to be grateful. I made you special. I made you popular. Your mom hates you; your whole family hates you. They'll never love you, they'll never forgive you. Without me you're nothing! No one will ever want to talk to you and the only way you'll ever get a boyfriend is by spreading those fat legs. Get used to being on your back because it's all you're good for. Get the hell out of my house!"

Molly sat frozen on the couch.

He threw her off the couch. "Are you deaf? Or just a freak? I don't want anything to do with you. You're a worthless ball of fat! You should find a dark hole and never come out. Better yet, why don't you just kill yourself and spare us all the horror of looking at you."

"I … You said you'd drive me home."

"Do you have money for gas? Dumb drunk freeloader. Do you plan to spread your legs to pay? Or is your mouth good for something besides eating?"

"How do I get home?"

"I DON'T CARE!"

Molly started sobbing.

"Oh god, I can't stand that noise! Shut your mouth and get out of here."

"What's going on down there?" a female voice yelled.

"Nothing!" Lance yelled back. "I'll turn the TV down, sorry!" He turned to Molly and hissed, "Get out."

Molly picked herself up off the floor, still sobbing. She grabbed her purse and scrambled up the stairs and out the back door. She stumbled to the curb and looked around. She knew there was a bus stop nearby and she thought maybe they had passed a convenience store but she'd still been buzzed on the beer Lance had given her earlier and too caught up in the music to pay attention to directions or landmarks on the way here.

She started walking just for something to do. At the corner there was a bus stop but a quick glance at the schedule told her she'd missed the last bus but at least she had a chance to review the route maps and find a bus that could take her to the mall. Ahead she could see lights.

A coffee shop or diner? She crossed the silent road and jogged up the block. The lights were coming from a 24-hour coffee shop that marked the end of the suburb and the beginning of the shopping district. She slipped inside under the drowsy gaze of the cashier. She scrambled through her purse, came up with a couple dollars in loose change, and ordered a hot chocolate so she wouldn't get kicked out. The place was empty but she chose a booth that hid her from the cashier and the windows and sat down.

It's too late to catch a bus, too late to call anyone for a ride, and no one would come anyways. Lance was the only person in the world who loved me and I ruined our relationship. If I went back and apologized would he forgive me? I wouldn't forgive me.

Her cellphone rang and her heart began to pound. *Lance!* She scrambled to get her phone out of her purse and panicked when she couldn't find it. It kept ringing and she started patting pockets. She had to half stand to rescue it from her back pocket and she hit the button without pausing to look at the call display.

"Hello!"

"Molly, thank god, is everything all right."

Her shoulders drooped and she slumped in the bench. "What do you want, Brandon?"

"I want to know you're okay."

"I'm not okay and it's none of your business. Why are you evening calling me? It's the middle of the night!" She hung up the phone and dropped it on the table.

Her thoughts swirled in a hectic mess and the beer she'd had earlier was making her stomach churn. She sipped at the too-hot hot chocolate in an effort to settle her stomach.

She picked up the cellphone again and started typing a text message to Lance.

"Baby, I'm sorry. I love you. I just got scared. It won't happen again. Will you forgive me?" She hit send and waited.

Five minutes later she was typing again. *"Lance, please don't be angry with me. I love you and I'll show you that I love you. Please text me or call me."*

Another five minutes and still no answer so she tried a third time, *"I'm sorry I made you angry. I never wanted to fight with you. Please call me. I miss you already."*

As she hit send her phone beeped and a 'low battery' warning popped up.

"Please. My phone is about to die. Please call me or text me."

The minutes ticked by in distressing silence interrupted only by the sounds of the night cashier puttering lazily behind the counter. The phone in her hands buzzed and powered down as the battery died. Molly tossed it in her purse and wrapped her hands around the mug of cocoa.

I ruined the only good thing in my life. What am I going to do without Lance? How will I ever be popular? Who's going to love me now?

The coffee shop door opened with a sharp jangle of the overhead bell. Molly's head jerked up; she ran a hand over her face. Her cocoa was now too cold to drink and a quick glance at the clock behind the counter told her she'd have to hurry if she wanted to catch the first bus of the day.

Molly didn't bus often but she knew how to get home from the mall so she gathered up her purse and hurried out. She met the bus at the corner and showed her student pass to the driver. The other passengers were mostly professional looking people on their way to work and none of them gave Molly a second look. She had to wait at the mall to transfer onto the empty bus headed for her little corner of the suburbs. She got off at the corner and walked the half a block to her house.

She passed Hank's car in the driveway but she was too tired to recognize that its presence meant something was amiss. She let herself in the side door and froze.

Her mom and step-dad were both talking on their cellphones in rushed voices and Shannon was on the cordless. For a good two minutes no one saw her and then her mom turned.

"Oh god, she's home. No, she must have just walked in." Joanna looked over her shoulder and yelled. "It's okay, she's back!"

Hank and Shannon began relaying the news into their phones.

Joanna quickly said, "I'll call you back," and rushed to Molly. "Are you okay, Sweetie?"

Molly said, "Yes, I'm okay," but her head shook a slow 'no'. "I didn't think you'd miss me yet. It's still so early."

"An extra shift came up at work," Hank said, joining them in the living room. "I got up to shower and saw your door was open. I went to close it so the sound of the water wouldn't wake you. Your bed was empty ..." He swallowed hard.

"I'm sorry," Molly said.

"Where were you? Joanna asked.

"I went to Lance's house."

Joanna pursed her lips. "Your boyfriend?"

Molly nodded, tears springing to her eyes. "But I don't know if he's my boyfriend anymore."

Her mother hugged her close. "Hush, it's okay. You're home safe and that's what matters right now. Why didn't you call?"

"My cellphone battery is dead," Molly said.

"Okay. We'll talk about the rest in a few hours." She kissed Molly's forehead. "I'm so glad you're safe."

CHAPTER 11

When Molly opened her eyes the house was silent. She stared at the deep purple curtains for a long time, watching the subtle play of light glowing through the textured fabric. From the amount of light peeking around the edges of the curtains and the deep, rumbling emptiness in her stomach Molly guessed it was around midday.

She sat up with a groan, still wearing the clothes she had come home in that morning. The alarm clock said it was after one. *With any luck the house will be empty,* she thought, opening her door.

Joanna was in the kitchen staring blankly at the front page of the newspaper her mug of coffee forgotten on the table. As soon as she saw her daughter she dropped the paper and stood up. "You're up. You must be hungry. I'll make us something. Are you in the mood for breakfast or lunch?"

"Uh, just some juice." Molly's stomach growled. "And maybe some toast?"

Joanna nodded. "Sure. Toast." She took a deep breath to steady herself and set to work. Toast and juice was effortless. Joanna would have rather whipped up a double batch of pancakes, or pulled out the waffle iron, if only so the mixing and frying could distract her for a short time. Instead her mind was free to dwell on the fears that had been eating away at her ever since Hank had shaken her awake.

"What do you want on your toast?" she said.

When there was no immediate answer she turned, worried she'd find the kitchen empty. *You're scared you're going to wake up to discover she never really came home,* the fear whispered inside her.

But Molly was there, sitting at the table, staring at her hands.

The toast popped, breaking the silence and Joanna said, "Molly?"

Molly raised her head slowly. "Just butter."

Joanna finished preparing the food and carried it to the table then sat down across from her daughter.

"I guess you want to talk," Molly said.

Joanna wanted to cry. *Her voice is small and frightened. Do I sound like that?*

"Mom?"

"Yeah," Joanna said. "We should talk. So, Lance. Who is he?"

Molly shrugged. "He's a friend of Trevor's; you know Kirsten's brother, Trevor, right? I met him over Spring Break. He lives on the other side of the mall."

"How long have you been dating?"

"Almost three weeks. But I think it's over now." She stopped when the tears threatened to overwhelm her.

Joanna reached across the table and took Molly's hand. "It's all going to be okay, you'll see."

"How could it be okay? The girls are going to think I'm a loser because Lance dumped me. Brandon hates me. School is a mess, and you guys …"

"We forgive you."

Molly pulled her hand free and looked away.

"I'm not saying that I'm not angry, Molly. You said some hurtful things and it sounds like you're fully aware of that. You scared us this morning, and you broke a lot of rules, so yes, I'm upset. But I still love you and I'm willing to forgive you. In time the anger will fade."

Molly nodded and bit into her toast so she wouldn't have to respond.

"You said you weren't sure if you two were still dating. What happened last night?"

"We fought. It was pretty bad. He wouldn't answer any of my text messages."

"Text messages? I thought you said your battery was dead."

"It died while I was texting Lance from the coffee shop."

"What coffee shop?"

"It's a few blocks from Lance's house. I went there after we fought to wait for the busses to start again."

"When did you get to the coffee shop?" Joanna was starting to sound panicky but she didn't care.

"It was about three in the morning I guess, maybe three-thirty."

"You walked through a strange neighbourhood to a coffee shop at three am, alone?"

"Yeah. Lance refused to drive me home. It was a really bad fight and he was really mad at me. I shouldn't have …" She stopped talking and picked up her glass of juice.

"Shouldn't have what, Molly? What happened last night?"

"Nothing," Molly mumbled against the rim of her glass.

"Molly, if something happened, if you're in any kind of trouble …"

"Nothing happened!" The thud of the glass slamming down on the table startled them both and they stared at each other, hearts pounding. Finally Molly said, "That's why it's over. I chickened out; I don't have what it takes to be cool. And now Lance probably hates me too."

Relief flooded Joanna and she felt her whole body relax. "It will all work out in the end. And sex isn't something you can take back so if you didn't feel ready then you made the right choice."

Molly just shrugged and nibbled at her toast.

"I'm happy you're home safe, Molly, but you did sneak out and you did scare us."

"You want to ground me again?"

"I'd like you to stay home this weekend, yes, but mostly because I'm terrified you'll disappear if I let you out of my sight. Silly isn't it?" Joanna tried to smile but her daughter didn't smile back. "Shannon is staying with Hank's parents so you don't have to worry about her bothering you all weekend. You can just stay home and take it easy."

"And that's it?" Molly hedged, hopeful.

Joanna took a deep breath. "That's it for punishment, yes. You're not going to be happy with this though."

"Why? What else?"

"Shannon tried to get onto your laptop, after we found you missing. A drink got knocked over …"

"Is it beyond repair?"

"No. Hank took it in this morning. You'll have it back in a week, or maybe less. It just needs to be cleaned."

Molly felt the anger and resentment building inside and closed her eyes. She wanted to know who was to blame; she wanted to scream that it wasn't fair. Instead Molly started to cry.

"But I'm not taking away your phone and if you need a computer for homework you can borrow mine."

"But no Facebook?"

"Not on my computer, no. I'm sorry Molly, it really was an accident."

"Fine." She pushed away from the table.

"Can I get you anything else?"

"No. I think I'll just go back to bed."

Joanna watched her daughter wander out and sighed. She set her empty coffee mug in the sink and picked up the phone. When Barb picked up she said, "Sorry for hanging up on you this morning."

"Understandable. How's our Molly?"

Joanna sat again. "I don't know yet. I don't know if I'll be dealing with the Molly I know or the monster teenager who's been living in my house this last week. Right now she seems tired and shaken."

"Give her time, Joanna. You remember how long it took you and your mom to reconcile."

"Is it really going to take that long?"

Joanna heard the chuckle on the other end of the line and then Barb said, "Who can say? Just be glad this boy is out of her life. Maybe the next one will be better for her."

"Are you still betting money on her and Brandon ending up together?"

"Who can say these days? I think their friendship got too strong for that. Maybe it's a good thing too. Friendships are harder to come by than spouses."

Now Joanna laughed. "You're a true cynic, aren't you?"

"Sometimes. You take care of your family and you call me if you need anything. Brandon and I are going out for lunch with my parents today."

"All right. You have fun and don't make your mom angry."

"Make up your mind! Fun, or angry parents? You can't have both you know."

Joanna laughed even harder. "I'll talk to you later, Barb." Shaking her head she hung up the phone. She hesitated in the hallway as she debated going to check on Molly. Finally she muttered, "Give her a little space all ready," and went downstairs to work.

Molly's cellphone was on the night stand next to her alarm clock where it had been charging all night. She grabbed it and crawled into bed. Even though her family had never been overtly religious she said a quick prayer to any god that might listen.

Please, oh please, let there be a message from Lance. That's all I ask. I just want to know Lance got my texts. Please oh please.

Nothing.

She sent another text. *"Lance, I'm sorry. I want to see you again. Please. Call me,"* then she lay back with a sigh and waited.

She stretched and rolled over, her gaze settling on the clock which now said two-thirty. She sat up with a jolt. *I fell asleep!* She fumbled for her phone which had nearly slid between the bed and the wall. *I missed him. He's going to think I'm ignoring him!* But there were no new messages and no missed calls.

She tried again. *"Lance, I'm so sorry. Can we try again? Can we at least talk?"*

She couldn't bear just sitting and staring at the phone all afternoon so she grabbed clean clothes and headed for a shower.

The hot spray washed away the last of the hung over fuzzy feelings but that left her emotions sharp and raw. She stood staring at nothing, not even noticing the tears until a pitiful sob escaped her lips. She clamped a hand over her mouth and cried until the water was too cold to stand under.

By the time her mother called her for supper she had sent four more text messages to Lance. All went unanswered. Molly sat poking at her food while her mom and step-dad ate and communicated in glances and facial expressions.

Finally Joanna said, "Are you feeling any better this evening?"

Molly shook her head 'no'.

"I know it hurts now, honey, but the pain does go away."

"You don't understand," Molly said.

"I do understand. My boyfriend dumped me over something I refused to do."

Molly couldn't keep the bitterness from creeping into her voice. "Yeah? And what was that?"

"I refused to get an abortion."

Molly looked up, meeting her mother's gaze squarely for the first time in days.

"I made the right choice for me, I knew that but I thought 'what's wrong with me for making this choice?' I knew if I had that abortion there was no bringing you back, no changing my mind. But if I had you and couldn't deal with being a mom I could always change my mind and give you up for adoption."

"But you didn't," Molly said. She had heard stories of those hard years when her mom had been in school and she had been a red-faced screaming baby but this story was new and she wanted every detail.

"No, I didn't. Labour was hard, just me and Barb and a nurse who openly disapproved of us two single teenagers. You didn't want to come out. And then they laid you in my arms and you squinted up at me and I knew I couldn't give you away. You were mine and I was going to keep you, no matter what. You were mine to love." She wiped tears from her eyes and squeezed Hank's hand.

"But you felt that way about Shannon too," Molly said.

"I loved her just as much as I loved you, yes, but it was different with her. Shannon was mine, but she was Hank's too, and yours. She was special because she brought us all together. You're special because you were only mine, you had no one else when you cried at night and I loved those long moments, even if the crying made me feel scared and insane."

They were back in familiar territory now and Molly found she was smiling. "You should have been used to all those temper tantrums then," she joked.

Joanna smiled too.

"Do you think Lance will go out with me again?"

"I don't know honey. If he's smart he'll respect your choice and give you another chance. If he's a jerk he'll take off without a backward glance."

Molly nodded. "I'm not that hungry."

"I understand. I'll pack the leftovers in case you're hungry later."

When Molly had gone Hank said, "You never told me that, about Rick wanting an abortion."

"I never told her either. It never seemed to be important, and for a long time she was too young."

"Why now?"

"I don't know. It felt like it was time. Do you think it made a difference?"

"It made her smile so yes, I do."

Molly's mood quickly soured. There was still no reply from Lance so Molly texted Kirsten. *"Lance isn't answering my texts. Can you convince him to call me?"*

She didn't have to wait long for a reply. *"I'll talk to Trevor. No promises but I'll try."*

There was nothing to do since her laptop was being cleaned and she didn't feel like watching TV since her mom would hover and fuss so she tucked into bed, hugging her cellphone like a child holding tight to a teddy bear, and waited.

She woke early Sunday morning and checked her phone. There was nothing new from Kirsten and still nothing from Lance. Leaving the phone she shuffled to the bathroom. Down the hall she could hear her mom and Hank saying their good-byes at the door. When she was done in the bathroom she shuffled to the kitchen where her mom waited.

"Good morning, Molly. Would you like some breakfast? I was just making some porridge."

"Just toast," Molly mumbled.

"Help yourself." While Molly made her breakfast Joanna kept talking. "I have a deadline coming up so I'll be downstairs most of the day. You're on your own for lunch."

"But you'll be mad if I skip lunch?"

"Mad? No. Concerned? Yes. You haven't eaten much this weekend, and you weren't eating much this last week or so. Unless Lance was buying you food at school?"

"No," Molly said and joined her mom at the table. "I just thought I'd lose some weight."

"Why? There's nothing wrong with your weight."

"I'm bigger than all my friends; I wear a bigger pant size than you do! I'm fat and you're not so it must be my eating habits, unless my dad was fat."

Mother and daughter stared at each other across the kitchen table for a long moment. In that moment Molly's anger fizzled and the doubt started creeping back in. For Joanna it was a moment of clarity, an answer to a question that had been bothering her since spring break; now Joanna knew how her wonderful teenage daughter could end up a rebellious delinquent.

"You're not fat," Joanna said, but her voice was hollow.

"I'm sure as hell not skinny either. So do I get that from my dad?"

Joanna fiddled with her coffee mug as she talked. "When your father and I were dating he was wiry. No, he was a bean pole. He got in a lot of fights because bigger guys thought he was weak, but he wasn't. There was nothing to him but it was all muscle, and he fought dirty. I watched him fight a few times; it was the most dangerous, exciting thing I had ever seen. Of course a lot of teenage boys are bean poles so he may have filled out since then. I haven't seen him since I graduated." She raised her mug to drink, then paused and set it down again. "That's not true, actually. I saw him in passing once or twice, across a crowded store, walking down the street, but he never noticed me, never acknowledged me. I don't even know if he recognized me. The last time I saw him I was shopping for Brandon's third birthday present. You were two and a half, and I had you with me in the store. I saw him and I thought, this is it, I'm going to introduce him to his daughter."

Silence hung heavy between them until Molly said, "Did you?"

Joanna shook her head. "I was going to, I wanted to, but then this young woman walked up to him, holding out a baby outfit and he smiled and took it from her and kissed her cheek. I don't know if it was a shower gift or if he was having one of his own, I just couldn't chance being rejected again. So I stayed in that row, out of sight, until they moved on, even though you were starting to squirm and trying to get out of the cart."

"Mom, I'm sorry. I didn't ..."

"It's okay, Molly. You have a right to know who you are and where you come from. I don't know where he is now, or how to find him. I can tell you that my grandmother was a bigger woman, my uncle was heavy too. Maybe it's just recessive, you know?"

Molly nodded.

"Did everyone tease you for being fat?"

Molly shrugged. "They didn't tease; not really, they just made it clear that I wouldn't be really cool and really popular unless I lost weight. I felt like being fat was my fault because you're so skinny."

"Do you think Barb is fat?"

"No."

"Barb looked a lot like you when I first met her. Just before she got pregnant she put grew an inch and instead of looking fat she looked curvy and down-right stunning, even in her pajamas." Molly crinkled her nose and Joanna smiled. "I'm serious, Molly. They were the worst looking, rattiest things you've ever seen but she made them look good."

"But I'm already as tall as you."

"But you're not quite as tall as I remember your dad. I bet you'll grow another inch before you turn 18, and then you'll be turning heads."

"I don't like people staring at me," Molly muttered.

Joanna smiled. "You know what, sweetie? I don't like people staring at me either."

For a moment Molly looked at her mom and the smile they shared was real and honest. Joanna drained her coffee mug. "That's my caffeine quota for the morning so I guess I'd better get to work. I'll be downstairs if you need me and I'll check on you later. Okay?"

"Yeah, okay. I have homework to catch up on so I'll be busy too," she lied. She waited until she heard her mom's footsteps going down the stairs before tossing her toast in the garbage and going back to her room.

There were no missed calls and no new messages. Throwing the phone into the wall was a bad choice, no matter how appealing it seemed, so Molly set the phone down on the desk and took several deep breaths.

Think Molly. You have to make him talk to you. You have to apologize and get him to forgive you before school tomorrow. You have to get his attention somehow so you'll talk to you.

The answer was so simple.

Molly took a deep breath and made a quick pass of the main floor. Her mother hadn't resurfaced. Feeling secure Molly crept back to her room and eased the door shut. She changed into the bra Lance had paid for and got her phone. Taking a full body selfie was harder than she expected and she took a dozen pictures before she was happy with the result. She texted the best picture to Lance with the message, *"I miss you,"* attached to it.

After ten minutes of waiting the doubts started nagging at her. *He already has a picture of me in my bra. He won't care if I send another. That was stupid! But what if I send him a picture he doesn't have yet?*

She leapt off the bed, flung off her bra, and went through the whole process of taking the perfect selfie a second time. This one she texted with the message, *"Call me"*.

Out of ideas all Molly could do was wait for the rest of the day.

CHAPTER 12

Molly wanted to stay home on Monday but she could tell her mom's initial relief had faded over the weekend and it wouldn't be a good idea to press for favours until the anger and hurt had faded too. *At least I got to eat this morning,* she thought as she got off the bus.

She was wearing her old clothes today. It didn't feel right to show up in clothes Lance had paid for right after their break-up fight. She would wear them again, they were hers after all, but not right away. She had done her make-up, it still wasn't as good as when Kirsten did it but she was learning and her mom wasn't protesting.

She rounded the corner, saw her friends, and smiled. *I'm glad I didn't ditch them like Lance asked. I could use some girl time, it'll help me get over him.*

They were huddled together giggling over something when Molly came up. "Hey ladies, what's the joke? I could use a laugh today."

Kirsten's phone disappeared into her purse and they all smiled at her. "Dance rehearsal mishaps," Kirsten said.

"We heard you had a busy weekend," Julie purred.

"Oh, how did you …"

"Facebook," Amanda said with a genuinely cheerful smile.

"And Trevor," added Kirsten.

"What did Lance say on Facebook? I was grounded."

Amanda was practically bouncing. "Oh, he said …"

Kirsten cut her off. "Nothing much, except that you two fought and broke up. How are you holding up?"

Molly shrugged. "It was a bad fight."

"You'll have to tell us your side," Julie said, eagerly.

When Molly frowned Kirsten said, "So we can stand up for you, of course. Who knows what sorts of horrible lies Lance will tell. We've got to run; we'll see you at spare."

The warning bell sounded and Molly had to rush to get her books together. She made it to the classroom door as the bell sounded only to find it empty, except for the teacher. He was obviously startled to see her.

"Uh, where is everybody?" Molly asked once the anthem was finished playing.

"They're off working on their projects. No one is required to be in the classroom until the presentations begin."

"Oh. I guess I'll go find Brandon."

"Molly, before you go, I want to talk to you."

If Molly's shoulders could have slumped any lower they would have. Defeated, she crossed the room to his desk. "I know I haven't been in class much lately but …"

"This isn't about the absences, Molly. You failed that last test."

"I was in a bad spot for a while. I was caught up …"

"With a boy, I know, I heard. That leads me to my next point. Brandon requested to work alone on his project."

"He did?" She should have sounded angry, or surprised, but instead she sounded small and pitiful.

"Pick any topic you want, get something done, and I'll give you the last slot on the presenter's schedule. It's the best I can do. Do you still have your booklet?"

Molly nodded.

"You can still pass this course if you put some real effort in on this project. Presentations start June tenth, be back in class on that day, I'll be taking attendance."

"Yeah. Okay. Thanks." She forced a smile and retreated straight to the girls' washroom. She turned on the tap and splashed water on her face. Her hands and knees were shaking and her breakfast sat heavy in her stomach.

He left me too. Brandon really hates me, just like Lance said. He was right about everything so he must be right about me too.

It was only when she turned the water off that she heard the retching sounds coming from the handicap stall. Dread settled over her already reeling emotions and she said, "Hello? Is everything okay? Do you need the nurse?"

There was a shuddery gasp for breath and then, "God, Molly, is that you?"

She recognized Kirsten's voice. "Yeah. Why are you purging during class?"

"I'm not. I mean, this isn't on purpose. I think I have the flu."

"Did you need anything?"

"Privacy." Kirsten sounded distressed.

Molly fled from the sounds of Kirsten vomiting.

Molly waited in the canteen, picking at her sandwich and ignoring the buzz of voices around her. When someone dropped onto the bench across from her she looked up to see Julie and Amanda with their lunch trays. Julie had soup and Amanda had a salad and they each had a bottle of water.

"Ugh, you're still eating bread?" Julie said. "Well then you can have my crackers." She shoved the packet across the table.

Amanda delicately picked the croutons out of her salad. "You look so sad, Molly. How are you holding up?"

Molly shrugged. "Everything's a mess. I feel like I'm... I don't know. It's just too much to deal with."

"You can stop poking the sandwich, I'm pretty sure it's dead," Kirsten said as she settled next to Molly with a bottle of water. "Crackers! Can I have those? This flu is driving me crazy. Maybe crackers will stay down."

"Go ahead," Julie said.

"So tell us what happened," Amanda said, excitement lighting up her face.

"I snuck out Friday night and went to Lance's house. We had a few beers and he started to get all touchy-feely."

"You made out?" Amanda squealed.

"Yeah, but it was more than that. He kept trying to stick his hand up my shirt."

"Lucky girl," Julie said.

"But we've only been dating maybe four weeks!"

"How long were you going to make him wait?" Julie asked.

Molly leaned back, confused. "I don't know. I just didn't feel ready. Waiting another week or two would be no big deal, right?"

"Right," Kirsten cut in. "He was totally out of line. Excuse me; those crackers aren't sitting well after all." Kirsten scrambled off the bench and walked as quickly as she could without running in the direction of the bathroom.

"We have an extra dance practice," Julie said. "I hope you get over him soon."

Amanda looked flustered for a moment then smiled at Molly. "It'll get better. We'll see you later!" She grabbed her salad and hurried after Julie.

Molly dumped her lunch in the garbage and went back to the library.

After school Molly walked with the crowd towards the bus loop, her head lowered. The noise of the other students isolated her instead of including her. The hand on her shoulder startled her and she spun. "Do I know you?"

The older boy shook his head. "Can I give you a ride home?"

"No, I have to take the bus. And I don't even know you."

"I'll drive you home and you can take your shirt off for me."

Molly took a step back. "Get away from me. I'm going to miss my bus."

"But isn't this you?" He held out his phone. The picture on the screen was Molly, topless, and the caption said, "Call me."

She scrambled away, her heart hammering, catching her bus just in time and collapsing, shaking, into her seat.

On spare the next day Molly went looking for Lance. She was ready to give up when she spotted him at a locker near the science labs. She jogged over.

"Lance, I need to talk to you."

He looked her over and sneered. "Are you going to beg? Or cry? Because we're over."

"Did you share those pictures?"

"Oh, that. I was wondering if you'd ever catch on to that. Yeah, I sent them to a few friends, why?"

"Some guy I don't even know asked me to take my shirt off for him!"

"Hey! You'll have a new boyfriend in no time."

"I want you to delete those pictures, all of them. And tell your friends to delete them too. You had no right to share them."

"And you had no right to take my money and then turn me down like that."

"I told you not to buy me things!"

"It didn't take much to change your mind."

"I thought you were buying me things because you liked me."

"Yeah, I liked you, but I was trying to fuck you. I thought you'd be easy but you turned out to be a waste of time. So I traded your photos for a few favours. One friend hooked me up with a lucrative job opportunity in exchange for those pictures. I had to get something out of our relationship."

Molly could only stare, her eyes wide and on the verge of tears.

"What did you expect? Did you think I loved you? Did you think I would date you for a few years and then get married and live happily ever after? This isn't a childhood fairy tale, you moron, and there is no way in hell you're a fairy princess. This was a high school fling! We would have stayed together for as long as the sex was good, or until I found something better. No sex, no relationship. You'd better get used to that. No guy is going to date you for you, Molly. If you want a boyfriend keep taking your top off, and start spreading your legs." He slammed his locker and sauntered off.

After a moment of frozen shock she chased after him. "Please, Lance. You have to get that picture back. Please!" She grabbed his arm.

He turned on her, tossing her to the floor. "Don't touch me. We're done. I want nothing to do with you. And even if I wanted to stop those pictures I couldn't. I don't even know how many people have copies now." He shook his head. "You're pathetic." And then he was gone around a corner leaving her in a shaking heap.

Molly scrambled to her feet and fled to the nearest bathroom.

Molly didn't come out of the bathroom until the lunch bell rang. She hurried through the crowded halls, her arms wrapped tight around her. She didn't look at anyone and she was convinced that every laugh was directed at her.

She found Julie and Amanda in the canteen with their sparse diet lunches and dropped onto the bench. "I have a big problem."

"Yeah, we know, you got dumped," Julie said. "How long are you going to be crying over that?"

"No! You don't understand!"

"Kirsten is sick," Amanda said.

"She has the flu, doesn't she?" Molly asked.

"No," Julie snapped. "She's lost control of the purging. She's throwing up everything she eats even when she doesn't want to."

Amanda's voice dropped to a conspiratorial whisper, "She's lost another five pounds, and that's in the last four days."

"I feel bad, I really do, but I need help."

"God, you're so selfish," Julie scowled. "Kirsten might be dying you know. She needs help, now. Real help for a real, life-threatening problem. Whatever little drama you think is so important really isn't."

"We thought Kirsten was your friend," Amanda said. They picked up their trays and walked away from the table.

Joanna woke Shannon at a quarter to seven like she did every school day. She made breakfast and braided Shannon's hair. Twenty minutes before Molly's bus was due she leaned down the hall and bellowed, "Up and at 'em Molly. You'll miss the bus."

She packed two lunches and called again. "Come on Molly! You can't be late!"

She checked that Shannon's agenda was signed and packed and then shooed her out the door to wait for her bus which always came first. With Shannon taken care of she went to bang on Molly's door.

"Molly? Are you out of bed yet?"

There was a muffled, "no" from the other side of the door.

"You need to hurry and get dressed."

"I'm not going."

Joanna opened the door. Molly was completely hidden under her covers so Joanna sat on the edge of the bed. "Are you okay?"

"No. There's a flu bug going around school. Kirsten was sick on Monday."

"Is it a runny nose or a sore stomach?"

"My stomach."

"I'll call the school and I'll make you some toast but then I have work to finish. You know where the Tums are, and where the food is. I'll check in on you around lunch time."

Molly stayed under the covers until she heard the click of a plate on her desk and the door closed again. She crawled out of bed because she really was hungry and, once the toast was gone, she crawled back under the covers to sulk.

It's not fair. I'm the one who said there was a problem with Kirsten. They're the ones who wanted me to throw up too. And I do care about her; I just don't know how to help her. They don't care about me; they wouldn't even listen to me. What am I supposed to do about the pictures Lance took? He wasn't supposed to show anyone! How could he do this to me? I loved him. I trusted him!

Molly's cellphone chimed and she peeked out from under the covers. The phone sat on the night stand beside her clock, silent again. With heavy limbs she fumbled for the phone and opened the message.

"Did the little baby stay home today? Or did you finally kill yourself? Good riddance."

Maybe breakfast was a bad idea, she thought as her stomach rolled. Another message appeared.

"I have some friends willing to pay for your address. If you're too tired to get out of bed they could come and keep you company.

Molly dropped the phone and bolted for the bathroom. The linoleum was refreshingly cool and after a few minutes of resting her head on the floor her stomach settled again. When her knees stopped quivering she pulled herself up and opened the medicine cabinet. The Tums were next to the general headache and pain medication and a miserable voice in the back of her mind said, *Pain killers, that's what you need. Take a bottle of pain killers and you'll never feel like shit again.*

She took down the bottle and stared at it for a long time. She rolled it in her hand and read the back. "For relief of headaches and minor body aches take one or two tablets every four hours as needed. Do not exceed six tables in twenty four hours unless directed by a physician." She rolled the bottle again, listening to the pills slide. "How many do you take to relieve a broken heart?"

A large handful should be enough. And why not? Lance hates you, he said so. The girls hate you; they won't help you when you need them. Brandon hates you; that's why he hasn't answered your email. Shannon hates you; that's why she hasn't talked to you all week. Hank's too busy to care about you. Your mom didn't care enough to catch on that you were faking sick. No one likes you. You failed everyone. You let them down. No one will miss you. No one likes you. No one will miss you.

The thought echoed in her mind, over and over, until she felt dizzy. Her head felt heavy, and thick, like someone had pumped it full of water.

You're a disappointment, a failure. You're better off dead.

"I'm better off dead," she whispered. She poured the smooth red pills into one shaking palm. Her mouth was suddenly dry so she filled the cup next to the sink with water. She stared at the face in the mirror, wishing again that she'd dyed her hair green.

"Good-bye."

The pills went in her mouth and she started to drink the water, trying to wash them down before she gagged. When they were gone she stared at the mirror again, her breathing ragged.

If I had that abortion there was no bringing you back. I couldn't give you away. No matter what you were mine to love. No matter what.

"Oh god," Molly whispered. She shoved two fingers as far down her throat as she could and dropped to her knees beside the toilet bowl. She felt hot and flustered and her head was spinning.

I'm not too late. I take it back. I want to take it back.

She gagged once, twice, and then her stomach heaved. She'd never been so happy to see her breakfast floating in the toilet. When her stomach stopped heaving she made herself throw up a second time, just to be sure, and then she drank two large glasses of water.

There was a light tapping on the door. "Are you okay sweetie?"

"I'll be okay," she called.

"Did you need anything?"

'Privacy,' was on her lips but at the last second she changed her mind and said, "No. I'm going to take a shower and try to sleep."

As soon as she was back in her room she turned off her phone.

She stayed in bed all day Thursday too. Her phone stayed off and she stayed away from the medicine cabinet.

CHAPTER 13

Molly was actually reading her last novel for English class, and enjoying it, when someone knocked at her door. "Yes?" she called, not looking up from the book.

Her door opened and her mom peered in. "I don't want to interrupt. Hank just got home and he brought this with him; it was done early." She set the laptop on Molly's desk. "Supper is in an hour. I'm making soup and sandwiches."

"Okay, thanks."

Molly tried to focus on her book but she kept glancing at the laptop. It had been five, almost six, days since she had been online.

"I can tell everyone my side of the story," she whispered. "I can tell Lance to stop sharing those pictures. I can check on Kirsten. I won't be on for very long."

She set the book aside and rolled out of bed. The laptop's start-up sequence took forever. Molly opened Facebook as soon as the system allowed and logged on.

The first post in her news feed was an album posted by Lance. It was titled: My Whore Ex-Girlfriend. She gasped. "Four-thousand-seven-hundred-eighty-three shares?" She opened the album. The shirtless photos were there, including the completely topless one she had texted him though he had placed black rectangles over her breasts. "Over ten thousand comments?"

She began reading the most recent comments:

"Send me the originals I want to see her tits."

"What a lucky bastard you are. How many times did you fuck her?"

"Now that looks like a girl who knows how to put out."

"Lance, man, where do you keep finding these sluts? I envy you."

The comments from the girls were just as bad:

"You've stooped to a new low."

"Did you really sleep with her? That's gross."

"She's fat!"

Molly scrolled back up to the pictures, her heart pounding so hard she couldn't think. There was something else, something she was seeing but not recognizing, something nagging at her. She blinked several times, trying to change what she was seeing.

He had tagged her name in each photo's description.

If I'm tagged any of my friends can see this. My cousin could see this. If she sees this and tells my mom ... She swallowed hard. *She's going to find out sooner or later.*

Molly found her mom and step-dad in the kitchen talking over coffee. From the doorway she said, "Mom, can I talk to you?"

"Hank and I were ..." she started but Hand cut in gently.

"This looks like it's more important than 'how was your day honey?'. We can get caught up later. Shannon wanted me to help her practice her lines." He came around the table and kissed Joanna's cheek. "Call us when dinner is ready."

Molly waited until she heard Shannon's door close. "Mom, I think I made a really big mistake." She pulled up a chair next to her mom.

"Is everything okay?"

"No." Molly broke down crying. Between sobs she managed to say, "I told him not to and he did it anyways. He said they were just for him but he lied. I didn't know and I sent him more and he shared those too."

"Shared what? Did what?" Joanna was close to panic.

"Pictures!"

Joanna was not naïve about the nature of the digital world her daughter was growing up in. *Details can wait. All that matters is Molly.* She slid her chair closer to her daughter and draped an arm over Molly's shoulders. The crying lasted a long time.

Finally Joanna said, "How many pictures and how bad are they?"

"He took three at his house and I texted him two more when I wanted him to forgive me."

"How bad are they, Molly?"

"I have my shirt off in all of them, just my shirt, except one where I took my bra off too." Molly buried her face in her arms.

"Does Facebook allow nude photos?"

"He censored them for Facebook but he's been texting them to his friends too."

Joanna took a deep breath and held it for a count of five before exhaling slowly. "Thank you for telling me. I'm not happy about this but you were right to tell me. I don't know yet what to do but we'll figure something out, okay?"

"Okay Mom," Molly said into her arms.

"Is there anything else I should know about you and Lance?"

"You were right; he did give me beer, sometimes at school."

Joanna took another slow deep breath. "Anything else?"

Molly shook her head.

"Why don't you help me make supper?"

"Okay Mom."

When Molly saw her mom waiting by the door Friday morning with her keys and purse in hand she didn't think her mom was waiting for her.

"Shannon's bus just left," Joanna said.

"I guess I'd better hurry."

"No need. I'll drive you today."

That stopped Molly short. Even when Hank wasn't working an early shift Joanna never drove either of the girls to school. Molly had hauled science projects and presentation boards on the bus many times over the last five years.

"Why?"

"Because we're going to have a chat with the principal."

Molly's heart sank. *Now she's going to find out everything I left out last night. There's no way she'll still forgive me if she knows everything.*

"Grab something you can eat in the car. Your lunch is on the counter."

Molly recognized the tone of voice and retreated to the kitchen for a brief moment of self-pity. When the bus had passed by without stopping and she could linger no longer she settled for a dinner roll for breakfast, grabbed the brown bag, and scooped up her backpack. "I'm ready."

Joanna nodded and led the way to the car. During the car ride and the wait in the office no words passed between mother and daughter. When they were finally ushered into the principal's inner office Molly sat in the chair and stared at the worn patch of maroon carpet between her feet.

"Thank-you for seeing us, Mr. Penner," Joanna said, shaking his hand. "I'm sorry I wasn't able to call ahead but the matter was only brought to my attention last night and I felt it needed to be dealt with immediately."

Mr. Penner's eyebrows arched. "You were previously aware of your daughter's truancies, were you not?"

"I was."

"Good. We sometimes have students pretend to be their parents, or have friends pretend to be their parents, to hide skipped classes and other disciplinary actions."

"This is more serious than skipped classes I'm afraid."

"By all means, I'm listening."

"I'm not sure if you were aware that there was a boy involved in Molly's recent change of behaviour."

"Lance Maher, yes. I caught them trying to skip class one morning and sent them back inside."

"Were you aware he was giving Molly alcohol on school property? I know she accepted it, and that's not good either. But she's a minor and I don't know how old Lance is …"

"He's nineteen. He's getting his hands on it legally I'm afraid, if it actually happened. Do you have proof?"

"Only that I smelled it on her breath one day, and she came home mildly intoxicated more than once. Molly could fill in the details, I'm sure."

Molly kept her eyes down and said, "He gave me a water bottle of beer the same day I was called to the office about my absences, and that Friday he gave me beer in his car in the school parking lot."

Mr. Penner frowned. "If Lance denies it this will turn into a he-said-she-said argument. Without proof there's not much we can do. We'll talk to Lance of course and remind him of school policy. If that's all ..?"

"No," Joanna snapped. "That is not all. Lance has uploaded half-naked pictures of my daughter onto the internet and is sending them via text."

"I'm sorry to hear that but we cannot reprimand students for actions performed outside of school."

"My daughter is a minor!"

"Your daughter and Lance were caught making out on school property. That we had proof of and that was dealt with according to school policy."

Joanna stared at her daughter. "Is this true?"

"Yes. But Lance was pushing himself on me. I tried to tell him no. And it never happened again. When the vice-principal said it wasn't allowed it didn't happen again."

"Which is why we didn't contact you, Mrs. Hammond. We felt Molly had learned from her error."

"Then why bring it up at all? So Molly let a boy kiss her at school, so what? Does that give him the right to post inappropriate photos of her online?"

"As I said before, there is nothing we can do about actions performed off of school property." He smiled but Joanna didn't smile back.

"There is one final thing. Molly will be readmitted into all of her classes."

"She's been removed for absences according to school policy. Besides, there is no way she could pass with the amount of work she's missed, all her teachers agree."

"If she's enrolled in a class and fails she can register for summer school, but if she's been kicked out she has to wait until next year, is that correct?"

"Yes, but …"

"So, you're going to give this sixteen-year-old who has never acted out before now a second chance to catch up on her education because you understand she was led astray by a boy. And you're going to do this because I'm going to report Lance to the police tomorrow and you want me to tell them you're doing everything in your power to help resolve this issue."

Mr. Penner actually went pale. "Of course. Molly will have to be on her best behaviour for the rest of the year."

"Of course," Joanna agreed.

"And we'll investigate those photos. Anyone caught with a copy at school will be dealt with accordingly."

"Thank-you," Joanna said, nodding.

"If Molly could just wait in the main office; it will take most of the morning to get her paperwork sorted out and to make up her work packets."

"Fine," Molly mumbled.

"And I will be back on Monday," Joanna said. "I will need summer school information and of course I want to keep you informed of what the police say about the case."

"Speak to the secretary, she'll pencil you in."

Joanna finally stood and held out her hand. "Thank-you for your time, Mr. Penner."

"Not a problem. I'm here to help."

Once out in the main office Molly slumped into one of the chairs. "We'll talk later," her mom said before turning her attention to the secretary. When her business was complete she turned back to Molly. "You're okay to bus home?"

"Yes."

"It's going to be overwhelming but do your best, all right? I'll see you after school." She hesitated, gave her head a little shake, and then left.

Sitting and waiting in the office was only marginally better than being in class. The big windows made her feel like some exotic animal in a zoo. *That's right, come gawk at the Blue-Crested Dumbass,* she thought as a group of girls paused and then hurried away, giggling. She sank lower in her chair.

The door to Molly's right opened and Mr. Penner stuck his head out. "Shirley, call Lance Maher down for me."

"Certainly."

The door closed and Shirley tapped a few buttons on her computer before turning to the intercom system. "Mrs. Cooper?"

The reply was faint and crackly. "Yes?"

"Is Lance in class?"

"No, he's not."

"If he arrives please send him straight to the office."

"Sure thing."

Shirley turned the intercom off and picked up the phone. "Mr. Penner? No, he's not in class. I'll let the rest of his teachers know. Yes, I'm almost finished. Okay, I'll call them next." As she hung up she shot Molly a sympathetic smile and went back to work.

When the bell rang for class break the halls filled up with students. Most of them were too busy talking to friends or rushing to class to notice her. Molly spotted Julie and Amanda with their gym bags over their shoulders. She waved, sitting up taller in her chair.

Amanda started to wave back but Julie said something Molly couldn't hear and Amanda dropped her half-raised arm. The crowd carried them out of sight. Molly sank even lower in her chair.

Shirley came over. "I've let your teachers know about the changes and they're working on your assignment packets. Your social issues teacher said you already had your final project so why don't you go work on that in the library. Just sitting here must be boring."

"Really boring," Molly muttered. *But maybe Brandon is in the library. Maybe I can apologize.*

"You can stay in the library for the rest of the morning," Shirley added. "Come back here at the start of lunch to pick-up your assignments. Okay?"

"Yeah, okay, thanks."

Another sympathetic smile and then the secretary went back to her work.

The librarian nodded to her as Molly came in. There were a handful of students spread between the computers and the work tables and none of them looked at her. Brandon was not among them. There were big windows along two of the walls here too but if Molly worked at the middle bank of computers she wouldn't feel like she was on display. She dug out her assignment, smoothing out a wrinkled page, as the computer powered up.

I don't know what topic to do. I didn't want to do this in the first place. At least working with Brandon was fun. Well, as fun as school work could be.

Instead of opening the internet she opened the school's inter-student email system. You could send an email to any account on any server, which was useful when you forgot a USB stick and had to finish an assignment at home, but you could only receive emails from other school accounts. Molly entered Brandon's school account and personal account in the 'TO' bar and started typing.

"I don't know if you'll read this or just delete it. I don't even know why I'm writing this. I messed up, didn't I? You were never the loser, I was. Lance was a mistake but it was my mistake to make. I just hope I didn't ruin your project. I'm sure you never want to see me again, so good-bye Brandon. Molly."

She hit send and tried to focus on her project.

Brandon didn't come in on his spare either. When the bell rang for lunch Molly packed up and went back to the office to collect her work. Mr. Penner was waiting for her. "You can eat lunch here today," he said, showing her to a meeting room next to his office. "After lunch you may attend your regular classes. Monday you may eat in the canteen so long as you continue to attend all of your classes. If you miss even one you will spend the next four weeks in this room. Are we understood?"

"Yes, I understand."

"Good. I will see you and your mom Monday morning." He went out, closing the door behind him.

The end of the day couldn't come soon enough. Molly sat through her afternoon classes, unable to concentrate on anything but the rolling in her stomach. She picked up enough fragments of gossip to figure out that Kirsten had been home sick since Tuesday making her entire dance class angry, including Julie and Amanda. She also heard her name, though that gossip was usually shared so softly that she couldn't pick out the details. From the sneers and the snickers she could guess at the words well enough.

On the way to the bus a voice in the crowd yelled, "Hey Molly! I'll give you a ride, and maybe even drive you home after!"

Taunting laughter followed her onto the bus. No one on the bus spoke to her but she was convinced they were all talking about her.

Her mom was waiting in the living room when she came in. "How much homework do you have?"

"A lot."

"Do you need any help?"

"Maybe with the math. I missed some notes."

"I can try to help you with the math," Joanna said. Both her daughters knew that math was not her strong point. "Or you can call Barb." She sighed. "Molly, come sit down, we should talk."

Leaving her bag by the door she came and sat beside her mother.

"I know you were really torn up when Lance broke up with you; how are you holding up?"

Molly shrugged, the question taking her by surprise. She had expected a hot-seat question-and-answer session, not this. "He made it pretty clear that we were over."

"You mean when you two fought at his house?"

"Yeah, and after."

Joanna nodded, not wanting to sound too eager for information. "So you've talked to him since the fight?"

"Yeah, just once, at school. He sent me a few text messages the day I was home sick but I didn't answer. They were pretty nasty."

"Do you want to talk about the fights?"

"No. It just hurts too much."

"Was that the only time you went to Lance's house?"

"No. I went one afternoon. That was the day you grounded me for a whole week. I guess I deserved that."

"Maybe, but I didn't like doing it. So, just twice?"

"Yeah."

Joanna nodded again. "Molly, is there anything else I should know about you and Lance? The police are going to ask a lot of questions and they're going to want a lot of details."

"That's really everything Mom. He bought me some stuff at the mall the other day: some clothes mostly and some make-up. He said he'd bought it because he loved me but later he told me he was just spending money to get … so I'd have sex with him."

"You'll want to make a list of everything he paid for while you were dating, just in case the police want to know. How physical was your relationship?"

"A lot of kissing, he liked to kiss me. And he touched a lot – my shoulder, my leg, my arm. I thought he was just being affectionate but sometimes it made me uncomfortable. I thought there was something wrong with me so I didn't tell him to stop. A few times he tried to get under my shirt."

"Molly, it's your body, it's your choice to make. You know I won't get angry with you if you and Lance had sex, but I need to know."

"We didn't have sex, okay!?"

"Okay, I'm sorry. Is there anything else I should know?"

"He transferred from another school during this school year. I don't know why. And I know where he lives."

"Okay. We'll give that information to the police tomorrow. Anything else?"

"No."

"Are you sure?"

"Yes! Can I go now?"

"I don't want to sit here quizzing you on every detail of your relationship, Molly! I can guess at how painful it would go over this again and again when it hurt so much the first time. But the police aren't going to be nice about this. The more they know, and the more I know, the more we can all help you."

"Fine. Can I go now?"

"Yes. Fine. Go. I expect you to make an effort on that homework."

"Whatever." Molly got up, grabbed her bag, and stormed off to her room.

Hank came out of the kitchen and sat beside Joanna. "Well, that sounded like it started out okay."

"Yeah, and then I'm left with the same snarling teenager I was dealing with a week ago! Where's my Molly?"

"She's still in there. She's come out a lot more this week. I know you have to push right now, but she's going to get defensive when you do. When this is all over we'll start patching things up with her."

"When will this all be over?"

"I don't know, Joanna. I really don't know."

CHAPTER 14

Joanna and Molly left for the police station early Saturday morning. Molly had never been to a police station before and there were so many different versions on TV that she didn't know what to expect. They walked into a boring receiving room with a few chairs, a chest high counter, and a lot of public safety posters decorating the walls.

The middle aged man behind the counter stood as they came in. "Can I help you?"

"My daughter is sixteen and there are nude photos of her online. She didn't put them there and we would like to press charges against the boy who put them up."

"Let me call one of the detectives to speak with you. Please, have a seat."

The chairs were hard and cold but they didn't have to wait long. A younger man in a dress shirt and tie came through a side door and smiled at them. "I'm Detective Price," he said. "I understand you have concerns about some online photos."

"That's right," said Joanna. "Nude photos of my under aged daughter."

"Come with me and I'll take your statements." Detective Price led the way to a conference room with more comfortable chairs.

"No interrogation room?" Molly said, looking around.

"No, not today," Price said with a smile. "Have a seat."

Joanna did most of the talking after that, only calling on Molly to confirm a date or relate a conversation. They went over the last two weeks in ever greater detail, pausing once when Detective Price offered to get them both a drink, until finally Price said, "Do you have copies of the photos?"

"I have the two I sent him," Molly said. "But he has all of them posted on Facebook."

"If I brought a laptop in here would you access the pictures for me?"

"Yes, if he hasn't deleted them."

"I'll be right back." He returned with an open laptop and set it down in front of Molly. "I'd like you to log into your Facebook account and access the photos for me."

Molly swallowed hard and nodded. Her fingers shook as she typed and she had to enter her password twice. Once online she navigated to the photos and turned the laptop back to Detective Price.

"Which ones did Lance take?"

"These three," Molly said, pointing out the ones from Lance's basement. "He may have taken more; he never showed them to me at the time."

"And you sent the other two?"

Molly nodded. "But he said the pictures were just for him."

"These pictures were posted on May third. Why did it take you so long to come in and report it?"

"I didn't have my laptop for a few days," Molly said. "I didn't know about them until Thursday night. No, that's not true. A boy confronted me with the pictures on Monday but I thought he was only texting them. I didn't find out about the online photos until Thursday."

"And you still waited until now?"

"That was my choice," Joanna said. "We went to Molly's school yesterday to settle some other problems. The principal, Mr. Penner, has already said he'll cooperate with you in every way."

"We really should have been your first stop in a case like this. The photos are out key piece of evidence and Lance or the Facebook administration could have taken them down at any time. Luckily for us no harm was done. I'll take this to our technician and he'll document the comments and save the photos into evidence. You'll have to stay off of Facebook for 48 hours or you'll bump him off your account. Depending on the nature of the comments they could be charged with soliciting a minor."

"What about the kids at school?" Molly said. "They keep saying rude things to me."

"Report them to your principal if you can. If the same person is persistent or approaches you off of school property report them to me."

"You can't make them stop?" Molly asked, sinking into her chair.

"No, not really. And most of them won't be charged. There's no crime in being a rude teenager. They'll get bored soon enough." He turned to Joanna. "We will need to document any personal messages exchanged between Lance and your daughter – both on Facebook and via text message. We'll also need a record of when the spoke on the phone. We can do this after getting a warrant to search Lance's records but it would be quicker if you gave us written permission to access the information on Molly's end."

"Anything to help nail the little prick," Joanna said with uncharacteristic bitterness.

"Then I'll be right back with the paper work. After that you'll both be free to go." He took the laptop with him.

Back in the receiving room Joanna glanced at the clock and frowned. "I didn't think filing a report would take this long. I wanted to take you out for lunch but I have to go pick up Shannon and take her to rehearsal. Can I schedule a rain check for tomorrow?"

"Sure," Molly said. "I have all that homework, remember?"

"As long as you remember to stay off Facebook."

"No problem there." Molly stared out the car window letter her emotions settle. *It's over now. The police will get rid of the pictures and everyone will leave me alone.*

The coffee shop was busy but not overly loud yet Joanna and Molly ate in silence. Molly watched the crowd, noting that many of the people in line were dressed in rough work clothes and took their orders to-go. The other sit-in patrons were a mix of elderly ladies chatting gaily, well-dress business types, and women her mother's age, with or without small children.

Joanna was watching Molly while her thoughts tumbled about her mind. There was so much to say, so many things to ask, and she didn't want to put Molly on the defensive. So where to begin?

"I think we need to make some changes around the house," Joanna said finally.

"What kinds of changes?" Molly asked, still watching a man in construction coveralls juggle four large coffees and a large bag of something. *Sandwiches? Or donuts?*

Joanna took a deep breath. "I think it's time you started helping out around the house a little more. And I think it's time I raised your allowance."

"How much helping out? And how much more allowance?"

"You'll still get your five dollars for lunch money every week and I'll give you twenty dollars on the first of the month in return for the chores."

Molly nodded. "Okay, what chores am I expected to do?"

"You'll do your own laundry, and the bathroom towels. And that includes washing your bedding every month. You'll cook supper once-a-week, and do dishes once-a-week."

"I can't cook!"

"Chicken strips in the oven, frozen pizza, even hotdogs or burgers, they don't take any special skill and I'll work with you if you need help or want to try something new. In a few years you'll be living in some dorm halfway across the country and I want to know you can cook more than instant noodles."

Molly smiled and shook her head. "Anything else?"

"You can help with the grocery shopping and you can do the vacuuming in your room. Just remember not to run the vacuum while Hank is sleeping."

"Okay, you have a deal. Is that why you wanted to take me out for lunch?"

Joanna sighed. "No, it's not. I feel like I'm losing you, Molly. I know I have to let you grow up and be independent but I had hoped we'd sort of go from being dependent daughter and bossy mother to a sort of friendship."

Molly stared into her mug as she swished the rapidly cooling liquid around, trying to mix the last of the chocolate syrup in and trying to find some sort of answer that wouldn't make her sound sappy.

Finally her mom said, "I guess part of the problem is my fault. I didn't realize how quickly you'd want to stretch your wings. And I'm terrified of you dating."

Molly nodded, still looking down.

"I want things to be better between us, Molly. I know they can't be the same but can we try to build something, some kind of friendship?"

"I think I'd like that," Molly said. "But I'm not too good at friendships. I just lost everyone who I thought was my friend."

"It's hard, I know, but being a teenager is one big learning experience. You just ran headlong into a mistake and it's painful."

"But I'll get over it, I know."

"I was going to say that you'll learn from it. You can wallow in guilt and self-pity or you can make yourself a better person."

"Well, I sure don't like who I am right now." Molly drained her cup and turned to the last of her sandwich more because it was there than out of any real hunger.

"I'm happy to see you're eating more."

Molly shrugged.

"I don't think you need to worry about your weight, but if you're worried then I'm willing to help you. Skipping meals isn't healthy but you can pick healthier options."

"I hate salads."

"Really? I didn't know that. What about fruit? Or raw carrots?"

Another shrug. "I like fruit, well, most fruit."

"There's nothing wrong with an apple for breakfast instead of porridge."

"I guess so."

"When you start helping with the groceries we'll be able to start buying more healthy foods that you enjoy. And we could check out a gym or something."

"Maybe."

"Have you talked to Brandon lately?"

Molly shook her head.

"What about the girls?"

"No. No one wants to talk to me anymore. And Kirsten is sick."

"You mentioned there was a flu going around."

"There wasn't. Kirsten has been making herself throw up and now she can't stop. They wanted me to try it but I didn't want to."

"You know, I never understood why you wanted to be friends with them in the first place."

"I guess I sort of fell in love with them, in a non-creepy kind of way. They were pretty and confident and I wanted to be like them, or at least be friends with them." Molly slid her sandwich back in its bag. "I'm finished."

"Okay." Joanna drained her coffee. "Then let's get out of here. There're too many people here anyways."

Molly nodded in agreement and they edged their way through the crowded doorway.

Joanna and Molly didn't have to wait at all when they walked into school Monday morning. Mr. Penner was waiting for them and ushered them straight in to his office. After a quick exchange of pleasantries Mr. Penner got down to business.

"We were contacted by a Detective Price this morning. He says he's in charge of the investigation into the pictures."

"Yes, that's who we spoke to on Saturday. I'm pleased that everything is moving along."

"We were able to give the detective the records he requested, both Lance's and Molly's."

Joanna simply nodded. "Good. And Molly's paperwork has been straightened out?"

"Yes, yes. And Molly and I have had a discussion about her expected behaviour and the consequences."

"And what's going to be done about the pictures already in circulation?"

Mr. Penner's eyebrows came together as he frowned. "The police are handling Lance and the photos, are they not?"

"Of course they are. But are you doing anything to stop the spread of those pictures? Can you be one hundred percent certain that not a single one of your students is viewing or sending those pictures while on school property?"

"That's not something we can control."

"All right, thank you. You have a good day today, Molly. I'm going to the newspaper to see if any of the reporters want to write a story on a high school that protects pedophiles. It was nice seeing you again, Mr. Penner." She looped her purse over her arm and stood.

Mr. Penner also rose. "Now wait just one minute! We are not protecting anybody. If students are caught with those pictures they will be dealt with."

"How?" Joanna pressed.

"Their phones are confiscated until the end of the day, as per the Electronic Device Usage Policy."

"And?"

"That is the extent of our school policy."

"You don't report them to the police? You don't inform their parents? What if this was a photo of a naked twelve year old rape victim that was circulating? What is it about Molly's situation that makes this excusable?" Joanna's voice was rising in volume and pitch as she spoke. "Do you feel Lance has the right to share them because Molly willingly took her shirt off for two of the offending photos? Do you think students in your school have the right to view them because Molly is sixteen and not twelve, or eight, or younger?"

"It's nothing like that."

Joanna sat again; her body angled forward, the perfect picture of attentiveness. "Then enlighten me. What would you do if it was the photo of a twelve year old rape victim?"

Mr. Penner cleared his throat. "We would call the parents and the police."

"My daughter is a minor. She is being sexually harassed by a boy who is legally an adult. I assume you will do what is right in this situation."

"Of course. Parents and police will be notified every time we find one of those photos on a phone belonging to one of our students."

"Or staff members," Joanna prompted.

"I resent that accusation."

"I don't give a shit," Joanna spat. "This is my daughter's reputation and future on the line. I want to know that you aren't protecting anyone who is violating her privacy."

"Should the unforgiveable circumstance arise, the police will be notified that a staff member is in possession of those photos."

Molly looked from her mom to her principal and back again. She'd never seen her mom act like this before but it made speaking out a lot easier. "What about the boys who keep asking me for … er … favours?"

"You'll have to report them," Mr. Penner said.

"I don't know their names. They just walk up to me at the bus loop. There are no teachers and I can't come back in or I'll miss my bus."

"You'll have to report them," Mr. Penner repeated. "We can't have a teacher shadow you everywhere, I'm sorry. How many times has this happened?"

"Twice," Molly mumbled.

Mr. Penner glanced over at Joanna then said, "Tell us about every incident, even if you don't know their names. We'll keep a record. It will help us to know how many copies we're looking for."

"Thank-you," Joanna said. "Since we're all agreed on what needs to happen, and we're all up to speed on each other's progress, I think I should get going. Molly, what class are you missing?"

"Social Issues, but we're just working on our projects; we don't have to check in with the teacher."

"I'll phone the library and tell our librarian to expect you," Mr. Penner said. "If you need anything further please just call the school."

Joanna forced a smile and stood. "I will do that, thank-you."

Mr. Penner showed mother and daughter out to the main office and shut his door behind them.

"You were pretty cool back there," Molly said.

Joanna smiled. "I'll see you back at home?"

"Yeah, I'll see you later."

By lunch time Tuesday Molly was ready for real human interaction. She'd been so caught up with her homework that the only people she'd talked to at school were teachers, the librarian, and Shirley in the office. Molly dodged through the crowded hallway making it to the canteen in record time. The line was through the door and every table was full because a rain storm had blown in and no one wanted to eat outside or walk to the convenience store down the road. It took several moments for Molly to spot Julie and Amanda in the crowd.

They were seated with their backs to the door and they were huddled very close together. Molly wiggled through the crowd and came up, unnoticed behind them.

Just as she was about to greet them Julie leaned away from Amanda to flick her hair over her shoulder and Molly saw what they were huddled over. They had Julie's phone out and a topless photo of Molly was on the screen.

Julie said, "I've been following the comments for days. This is hilarious."

"You guys knew about the pictures?" she said.

Amanda had the decency to blush and look ashamed but Julie just glared at her. "Of course we knew about them. We don't get grounded and kicked off of Facebook."

"I wasn't grounded, my laptop was in for repairs," Molly said. "That's beside the point. How come you didn't tell me about them? How come you're following the comments? Why aren't you helping me get them taken down?"

"Take them down?" Julie scoffed. "Yeah right. I don't want to make Lance angry, he's cool and you're nothing. Excuse us. We're having lunch."

"Amanda?" Molly pleaded.

Amanda glanced at her with big eyes then looked back at her lunch tray. "Sorry Molly."

Molly was crying now and didn't care that people were turning to look. "You two are horrible people. I trusted you! You said you were my friends and you weren't. You were supposed to watch my back, that's what friends do!"

"Like you watched Kirsten's back?" Julie taunted.

"I told her to stop. I said it was a bad idea! You wanted me to try it!"

Julie rolled her eyes. "Of course we wanted you to try it. We wanted you to feel bad about your weight. We were trying to hurt you, Molly. Now get lost."

There was nothing to say that didn't sound childish so Molly stormed out, shoving her way through the gawking crowd.

CHAPTER 15

At home that afternoon Molly found no consolation on Facebook. Everyone was so concerned about Kirsten's condition and no one responded to any of Molly's status updates, except for one of Lance's friends who told her to shut up. She kept receiving updates saying someone had commented on a photo she was tagged in, a continual reminder that everyone was staring at her and making fun of her.

She had informed Mr. Penner of the photos, and given him Julie and Amanda's names, but she had no way of knowing if either girl was paged to the office that afternoon. Both had removed her from their friend lists so she could no longer see their status updates.

There was no word from Detective Price on the case either. Lance hadn't posted anything about being contacted by the police and the photos were still up.

A personal message popped open on her screen. *"Meet me at the park. I want a blow job. I can pay."*

She closed it without responding and logged off.

The next morning she walked into the kitchen in her pajamas and said, "I'm not going to school."

Joanna was busy packing lunches. "You have to go to school or they'll kick you out."

"Julie was laughing at the pictures at lunch yesterday. My own friends are sharing the pictures. No one is doing anything to stop the harassment. I can't go back. Mom, please, I can't go back."

Shannon frowned. "What pictures?"

"It's nothing, sweetie. Go get dressed and then I'll do your hair."

Shannon huffed but did as she was told.

"Your school work …"

"I'll do it from home," Molly snapped. "But I'm not going back. Pull your scary mom act and tell Mr. Penner that it's his fault I can't be in school. I can't go back. They're all looking at me and asking me for … for nasty things. I can't face them."

Joanna's face was deadly serious and she nodded once. "Fine. I'll call. But you'll be doing homework and chores during the day. I won't have you moping about doing nothing."

Molly just spun on her heel and stormed back to her room.

Molly spent the rest of the week in self-inflicted exile. She came out to eat only when she knew the kitchen was empty. She did her chores while her mom was downstairs working. She spoke to her mom only when spoken to. The only other person she would speak with was Detective Price who called Thursday to explain that the photos had been left up as a way to catch as many people soliciting a minor as possible.

"It will make it easier to charge Lance," he explained. "We can show a judge just how much damage this one act has caused. That's why we haven't spoken to Lance yet. We don't want to alert him."

By Saturday she was going stir crazy, alone in her room with a pile of homework that she didn't feel like doing. There had been no further word from Detective Price. Facebook made her more miserable every time she looked at it. And Brandon hadn't returned her e-mail.

On Monday afternoon Joanna said, "Molly, I have to help with Shannon's school play after school today. Your list of chores is on the table. There's also a shopping list. Please have the groceries home before supper time, I need the milk."

"Fine," Molly said.

Joanna frowned but said nothing as she grabbed her keys and purse. "The fresh air will be good for you."

"Sure."

Two hours later Molly stood in the junk food aisle at the corner store eyeing the pretzels and fingering the money in her pocket. Today's chores included picking up a few things at the grocery store while her mom was at Shannon's school helping with school play preparations and her step-dad slept off a week of double shifts. The store was a little place four blocks from Molly's house that stocked the necessities, like bread and milk, as well as some dry and canned goods and a lot of pop and junk food. There was a freezer in the back corner filled with pizzas and burritos and a slushee machine near the front.

She already had everything on the list but she wanted to sneak in a snack.

The sandwich meat was on sale, she thought. *And Mom would have given me a little extra for just in case. There's probably enough. There should be enough. If there's not enough I'll just ask the cashier to put the pretzels back.*

She reached for the bag as two older boys turned down her aisle.

"Are you sure?" the taller one asked.

Molly ignored them and tucked the pretzels carefully into her basket.

"Of course I'm sure. How many girls have their hair cut like that?"

Molly's head snapped up and she realized, too late, that the boys had stopped right behind her.

"Are you Molly?" the tall one said.

Molly's knees trembled, her hands gripped the basket white-knuckle tight, and her mouth went dry. "I don't know who you are."

"We'd like to be your friends," said the shorter one with a grin. Molly noted that he had movie star teeth. It didn't make his grin any less creepy.

"I'm sorry. I just want to be left alone." *I can't get past them. Whichever way I go they'll just block my path. It's like how Hank used to tease me and Shannon by blocking us in the hallway until we just crawled under his legs.*

Just the idea of going down on her knees in front of these two, for any reason, disgusted her so badly that her stomach rolled.

"That's not what we heard," said Creepy-Grin, taking a step closer to her.

Molly's back bumped the shelves and she glanced at one and then the other and then back again.

"You should be good to us, like you were for Lance," Tall-Boy said.

"I didn't …"

"My car's outside," Creepy-Grin pressed. "We'll give you a ride home, too."

"No."

"It's kind of cute that you're all nervous about this," Creepy-Grin said, reaching out to touch her cheek. She jerked away.

"Lance told us how much he spent on you to get you to put out," Tall-Boy said, grabbing her wrist and shoving some crumpled bills in her hand.

"I don't know what you're talking about," Molly said, looking down at the money in her hand. When she looked up again Tall-Boy planted his lips firmly against hers.

Her body went numb. The money fluttered out of her limp fingers. The basket hit the floor. The eggs cracked and leaked yellow.

"Hey you kids cut that out!"

Tall-Boy jerked back and Molly ran.

She heard the clerk call after her but she didn't stop.

She nearly collided with a cart that appeared suddenly at the end of the aisle. The cart's driver, a prim, elderly woman, scowled and snapped, "Slow down! You teenagers are all same. Nothing but a bunch of inconsiderate, reckless, hooligans."

The angry words chased Molly out of the store, her exit punctuated by a sarcastically cheerful door chime.

The blocks between the store and home passed in a blur of tears. She crossed three intersections without encountering any traffic and ran blindly through the fourth, not hearing the blaring of angry horns. The house was silent when Molly careened through the side door. She went straight to her room, slammed the door, and dove into bed.

Finally, after a lot of crying, her feelings of fear and humiliation faded to a numb ache. Feeling empty she rolled out of bed and went to her computer.

Someone will care. Someone will tell me it's okay. I can yell at Lance, maybe now he'll take the pictures down. Maybe ...

Molly's pictures were still on Facebook and there were dozens of new comments. Girls laughed at her; boys made lewd suggestions. And then she stumbled across a comment from Lance.

"I had to drop a lot of money on this one but in the end it was worth it. There was one hell of a sweet prize between her chubby thighs. If you want a kinky ride this is the slut for you. She couldn't get enough of me. Her favourite word is 'more' and she never says 'no'. Seriously, this girl is desperate for sex."

Molly could do nothing but stare for a long time. Then she reread the comment but its contents were the same. She read the comments after Lance's but didn't recognize any of the names, not until she came across Julie.

"Molly is pathetic. I can't believe we were friends. She's a loser and she always will be. She can't even sleep her way to popularity."

Molly clicked back to her news feed. She didn't see the update on Kirsten's bulimia. She didn't see the concerned note from her cousin. She clicked the status update box and started to type.

The trip to the bathroom didn't take long. Neither did the trip to the kitchen. She had everything: water, headache pills, back pain pills, and Hank's prescription sleeping pills. She took one of each and washed them down. There were two new comments on her photos and nothing on her status. Three more pills. A personal message popped up asking her for a blow job. Three more pills.

This won't take long at all.

Brandon let himself into the apartment, dropped his bag on the floor and dropped onto the couch. He had four classes this semester: Social Issues, Electronics, Science, and Math. The Science and Math weren't so bad but he had major projects in the other two classes.

And it's your own fault you decided to scrap the drug project to do something different. You're just luck you were able to move back your presentation date.

Brandon's every spare moment was spent in the electronics lab where he could work on either project as time, resources, and inspiration dictated. He'd even taken to eating his lunch there. He wanted to take a break, or maybe even a nap, but he had too much work to do.

I'll just check Facebook to see how bad the comments on her photos are getting. And then I'll check my e-mails because I haven't done that in a week at least. And then I'll get down to work.

While the computer powered up he fixed himself a snack and read the scrawled note on the fridge telling him when his mom expected to be home from work. He logged on to Facebook and found a status update from Molly.

"*I'm fatter than society wants me to be, that's what started all this. I wanted to be popular and I let a boy convince me that he could make me popular. I let him talk me into making a lot of mistakes. The worst mistake was taking my shirt off for him. Now he's shared the photos and everyone can see how fat I am. Everyone is either making fun of me or asking me for sexual favours. They don't understand. Lance and I NEVER had sex. Lance is a jerk. He tried to use me and when it didn't work he chose to humiliate me.*

"*Everyone thinks Lance is cool and I'm the loser. I have no one left. My friends all hate me. The cops can't help me. The school won't help me. My parents can't stop random boys from trying to buy sex from me. Lance is threatening to give people my address. Soon I won't even be safe at home.*

"*Two boys cornered me at the grocery store today. They shoved money in my hand and one kissed me. I didn't want him to kiss me. I never want another boy to kiss me ever again. I hate boys. I hate kissing. I hate dating. And I hate myself.*

"*No one can help me. No one can stop this. I can't do this anymore. I can't deal with the harassment anymore. I don't want people staring at me and laughing at me.*

"*No one will see this. No one will care. No one cares about me. No one will miss me.*

"*Mom, I'm sorry.*

"*By the time anyone notices this I'll be dead.*"

Brandon's heart was pounding. He wanted to reread the update again, he wanted to sit and stare, he wanted to find Lance and strangle him.

No time. There's no time. Please, don't let me be too late.

Brandon grabbed the phone and dialed Molly's number from memory. It rang over and over as Brandon paced. "Please pick up. Please pick up." When the answering machine kicked in he hung up and redialled.

This time the phone picked up and a sleepy male voice said, "Hello?"

"Hank, this is Brandon. Molly just posted a suicide note online. I'm calling an ambulance."

Hank heard the phone and buried his face in his pillow. *The answering machine will get it.* When the ringing stopped he sighed and tried to settle to get a few more hours of sleep before his next double shift. Then the phone started again and he groaned.

"Hello?" he mumbled once he got the bedside phone off the hook.

"Hank, this is Brandon. Molly just posted a suicide note online. I'm calling an ambulance."

The receiver dropped from Hank's hands and he was out of bed in a heartbeat. He raced down the hall and slammed Molly's door open.

"Molly!!"

CHAPTER 16

There was an unfamiliar beeping noise. It was faint but piercing and very distracting. Every time she would relax and start to drift on clouds of unfeeling freedom there would come another beep. The beeping became louder and sharping and the clouds drifted away leaving nothing but cold blackness. Beyond the blackness she heard murmurs, like people talking in another room. The voices came and went, too distant for her to hear any words, and with them the constant beeping.

Alone in the black she tried to think but even though she couldn't see the clouds anymore her mind felt foggy. She remembered only fragments that made no sense together. Faces but she couldn't always remember names. Words but she couldn't recognize voices. Conversations with too many missing pieces; events jumbled together out of time.

Time. How long had she been alone in the darkness?

Her eyes opened. It was dark but not as dark. There were no voices. There was a light somewhere, strangely coloured, and the beeping. She became aware of her own body, the heaviness of her legs, the beating of her heart, a pinching in her arm when she tried to lift it, and the weight of something draped over her body.

Thoughts formed. Questions. *Where am I? What time is it? Why doesn't that beeping sound just stop so I can sleep?*

Voices, distant. She tried to call to them but her throat didn't want to work. She swallowed and tried again. A rasping, "Hello?" escaped her lips.

There was movement closer than the voices.

"Hello?" she tried again, a little stronger this time.

"You're awake," said a voice, clear and close and so familiar she ached to recognize it.

She turned her head. There was a person there, a lady, a familiar lady. She blinked a few times, focusing intently on the face. Her memories were in a jumble but this face was in so many of them. A scrap of memory floated by: this face, smiling, and her own voice saying, *mom*.

"Mom?"

Her mom nodded. "Yes, I'm here. The nurse will be here right away. They weren't sure when you would wake up."

"Nurse?" She closed her eyes and took a deep breath. When she opened them she turned her head slowly from side to side. The light was a screen with numbers on it and the beeping was coming from the screen. The bed was narrow with rails on both sides. There was a curtain behind her mom and a TV on one wall. *Definitely a hospital*, she thought. And then, without warning, another thought drifted through her mind. *I guess it didn't work.*

Just then the nurse came in. She took Molly's wrist and looked at her watch, then at the screen. She smiled. "How are you feeling?"

"Confused," Molly said. "Thirsty."

"I'll get you some water. Remember to drink slowly. The confusion should clear on its own in the next day or so. And your mom is here to help you."

Molly nodded, feeling too scared to be reassured by the nurse's kind demeanour.

Molly's mom said, "Do you remember anything?"

Molly just shrugged.

The nurse came back with a plastic cup, complete with lid and straw. "Here you go dear. If you need anything else your mom can press the button. You should try to go back to sleep for a few hours, it will help with the confusion.

Molly nodded again and took the cup. Her hands were shaking and she was suddenly grateful for the lid. She sipped slowly at her water, painfully aware of the silence broken only by the beeping of the heart monitor. Finally she said, "Why am I in the hospital, mom?"

Her mom tried to smile. "The nurse is right, you should try to rest. The doctor will be in to check on you in the morning. He can fill you in then."

"Oh. Okay." She took another sip of the water and handed the cup to her mom. She closed her eyes, even though she wasn't sure she was tired, and let her mind drift through the blackness.

The fragments were larger, more cohesive. She saw Kirsten and Julie and Amanda smiling sharp smiles; they were in the hallway at school. She saw Brandon in the library, his face was hard. *"Get out,"* he said. She saw Lance smiling at her and then his smile vanished and he was screaming too. *"Get out! Get out!"*

Why are they all so mad at me?

She saw Shannon in tears, heard her own voice: *"I hate all of you!"*

She saw Lance again, handing her a beer. *"Don't be a loser Molly. It's just harmless touching."*

She remembered Lance kissing her and trying to touch her. She remembered the fight with her mom and step-dad. She remembered Shannon screaming at her, *"You're the worst big sister ever!"* She remembered being slapped and thrown off the couch. He had kicked her out, pushed her aside as if she meant less than nothing. She remembered the pictures.

And she remembered the stranger in the grocery store, bigger than her, stronger than her, and unwilling to take no for an answer.

I went home and found the pills. I tried to stop the pain. I guess it didn't work.

When she opened her eyes again it was morning.

There was a strange man with a clip board standing beside the bed and she guessed he was the doctor. He smiled at her and put his pen under the clipboard clip. "Good morning Molly. How are you feeling?"

"Why am I here?"

He continued to smile "The nurse mentioned you were feeling confused. Do you remember anything?"

"I remember everything. Why am I here?"

"They had to bring you to the hospital so we could pump your stomach. It's been a week since you overdosed. We saved your life."

"Who said I wanted to be saved!? I wanted to die! I want to die! Why didn't you let me die?" She was sobbing now and the beeping was getting faster.

"Molly, you need to calm down. I know you felt that way when you took the pills, and maybe you feel that way this morning, but someday you may change your mind. You have a lot of life ahead of you."

"I don't want it."

He smiled again. "Now that you're awake I'll make an appointment for you to see the hospital psychologist."

"I don't want to see a psychologist. I don't want to be here."

"I can't sign your release papers without an 'okay' from the psychologist."

"I don't want to be HERE! I don't want to be alive! Living is too damn painful, do you understand that? I'm worthless. Everybody hates me. I just want to die."

"I'm sorry to hear that." He scribbled a note on the clipboard. "I'll check in on you in a few hours. Try to stay calm, okay? You need to stay on the IV today but you can have water and juice. Tomorrow morning we'll pull you off the IV and you can eat on your own. Your family is here to see you."

"I don't want to see them."

"They've been waiting for you to wake up."

"I don't care."

"They do. I'll be back. Just press the button if you need anything. The nurses are very understanding."

She wanted to scream at him for smiling at her like that but he turned and left and her mom and step-dad came in.

"Hey sweetie," her mom said. "How are you feeling?"

"I want to die."

Her mom's smile faltered.

Hank said, "It's been raining for about eight hours now, on and off." He pulled up a chair. "Big thunder and lightning show last night.

Shannon loved it. She got a little angry when we wouldn't let her play out in the rain. She was so excited to go out in the puddles today."

"I don't care."

He kept on talking, his voice even, almost emotionless, and his eyes on his hands. "She's staying with her grandma for a while, she'll have fun there. My mom loves kids. She and Shannon are going to bake cookies. She wanted to come today but we didn't know if you'd be awake yet. Now that you're awake she'll want to see you, or at least send you cookies."

"Why are you telling me this!?"

He looked sad all of a sudden. "Because I don't know what else to do."

When the doctor returned the next morning he had a young, professionally dressed woman with him. "Molly, this is Dr. Karen, she'd like a chance to speak with you."

"I don't have a choice, do I?" Molly muttered.

The two doctors exchanged glances. "No," Dr. Karen said. "Not really. But you do have the choice of what to tell me. And how much you want to tell me."

"But if I don't answer all your questions I'll be stuck here."

"I have other patients," her regular doctor said, stepping out and leaving her alone with the psychologist.

Dr. Karen settled in the chair next to the bed. "I know you don't want to talk to me and I know you're probably tired of listening to people tell you how you should feel and what you should do, but until you decide to talk to me we're in a stalemate. This is up to you, Molly."

"Then why didn't they let me die?"

"Because people are selfish. The people who love you don't want to lose you; they can't understand the pain that drove you to take all those pills, all they understand is how much they would miss you."

Molly sighed. "I just wanted to leave all the pain behind. And now I'm stuck here with all the pain and everybody's pity too."

"Molly, why did you try to kill yourself?"

Molly looked away.

"Was this the first attempt?"

"No."

"Tell me about the first time."

"I had a fight with my ex-boyfriend. The next day I tried to over dose but I got scared and made myself throw up."

"It's never that simple, Molly. What did you two fight about?"

The question was met with sullen silence.

"Where did you fight?"

"At school, in the hallway."

"Was this your break-up fight?"

"No."

"Why did you break up with him?"

"I didn't .He dumped me because I wouldn't sleep with him. Okay? I don't want to talk about Lance. I don't want to think about Lance. He hates me, and now everyone else does too."

"Why do you think everyone hates you?"

"Because they're making fun of me and harassing me and because no one will help me."

"Help you with what?"

Molly shook her head.

"Molly, remember that we can only get through this if you talk."

"I don't want to talk about that."

"Then let's talk about Lance. Tell me all about your relationship with him."

"We met at the pool. He's a friend of my friend's older brother. He's older than me, I think he said nineteen. He liked me. He paid attention to me instead of to my friends like all the other boys do. He would kiss me and tell me I was beautiful. He bought me clothes and make-up and food. I thought he really cared about me."

"How many times did he ask you for sex?"

"It only got that far once. He would kiss me; sometimes it was a lot of kissing. Sometimes I wanted him to stop but mostly it was really nice."

"Why did you sometimes want him to stop?"

"I don't know. It just wouldn't feel right anymore."

"Were there other times that you got that 'not right' feeling?"

"Sometimes he'd ask me to do things, like drink beer or skip class, but I did it anyway because I wanted to be popular."

"So you went along with him because you wanted to be popular?"

"Yes."

"Do you think drinking beer and skipping class would make you popular?"

"I don't know. Being me wasn't working so I thought I'd let Lance make a new me so I could be popular."

"So why didn't you sleep with him?"

"Because I didn't want to; I wasn't ready."

Karen nodded. "So he dumped you and later you two fought. What were you fighting about?"

"I don't want to talk about it."

"You'll have to talk about it eventually Molly, but for today we can stick to subjects you're more comfortable with."

They went on to discuss Molly's friends, Kirsten, Julie, Amanda, and Brandon. Molly didn't like all of the questions and sometimes lied about the answers. She didn't want Karen to know that she really did miss Brandon. She didn't want Karen to know how badly the girls had hurt her. She didn't want to admit that she still cared about what happened to Kirsten even after the girls had been so mean to her.

Finally Dr. Karen stood up and stretched. "That was a good first session, Molly. I will be back tomorrow to talk again. There's something I want you to think about until then."

"What is it?"

"I want you to think about what being popular means, and what price you'd be willing to pay to get it. I think you have a visitor."

Molly's eyes went to the door and she scowled. She turned to the window with her arms crossed.

Brandon's smile was sheepish and he nodded to the psychologist as they passed each other. He hovered near the bed. "Hey Molly. I'm glad you're all right."

"I'm not all right."

His smile faltered. "I, uh, got your e-mail."

"So why didn't you reply? I waited for more than a week! I thought you hated me, just like everybody else. I kept looking through the comments on Facebook expecting to see your name there."

"I don't hate you, Molly. I was so busy with projects that I put off checking my e-mail for over a week. I'm just glad I checked Facebook first on Monday."

"What day is it today?"

"Monday again. It's the long weekend."

Molly nodded.

"Is there anything you need? Clothes? Better food?"

"I don't get to eat anything until tomorrow so I don't know how bad the food is, but clothes would be good. This hospital gown is stupid."

"Okay, I'll tell your mom." They sat in awkward silence for a long time before Brandon said. "You know, small talk is harder than it looks."

"You could just leave," Molly said.

"The thought never crossed my mind."

They ended up sitting for close to an hour, saying very little to each other. Molly had so many questions she wanted to ask about the week she had missed but she didn't really want to hear the answers so she kept quiet instead. Brandon wanted to hug her and tell her over and over again how happy he was that she wasn't dead, but she'd only just forgiven him, maybe, and he didn't want her to hate him again.

When the nurse came in to do Molly's blood work Brandon said, "I'll come back in a few days, okay?"

"Don't trouble yourself," Molly replied.

"It's no trouble at all," Brandon shot back with a grin.

Molly just looked the other way until the nurse was done with the needle vials.

Tuesday morning she sat through her mom's visit in sullen silence with her arms crossed over her chest. Dr. Karen came in after lunch and asked, "How are you feeling?"

"I want to die."

"Physically, how are you feeling? Any aches or pains? Do you wake up feeling groggier than normal?"

Molly shrugged.

"Nothing's standing out so that's a good sign at least."

"I don't want to talk to you."

"We're not going to talk about you, Molly. We're going to talk about popularity. What is it that makes a person popular?"

Molly shrugged. "Lots of people like them."

"You're right. Popular actors are the ones with lots of fans and who make lots of movies. Popular singers have lots of fans and have lots of songs on the radio. But do high school students have fans?"

"No."

"So they have lots of friends?"

"Not really. Kirsten only really had a few friends that she hung out with all the time, but people liked her."

"How do you know?"

"They talked to her in class, and in the halls. They replied to her posts on Facebook."

"Okay. So popularity is determined by your level of social activity. What about the cost of popularity?"

"I don't know."

"Let's talk about celebrities again. What happens to a lot of popular artists?"

"They do crazy stupid things that get them in trouble. But they have all that money."

"Very true. So Kirsten and Julie and Amanda never do stupid things?"

"Kirsten is bulimic," Molly admitted. "But what does that have to do with popularity?"

"What do you think?"

Molly did think about it. She remembered Kirsten patting her thigh and saying 'You don't want to end up fat and alone, do you?' and 'last week my jeans were snug so I thought, I'll just purge once or twice more, just to stay in shape'. "Kirsten was afraid of being fat. She was afraid that if she gained weight she wouldn't be popular."

"Would you still want to be popular if it meant throwing up every day?"

"I didn't purge."

"But if someone said that it was the ONLY way to be popular, would you do it?"

Molly shook her head. "I couldn't. Throwing up when I took those pills was bad enough. I hate throwing up."

"So there is a price to popularity and it's pretty steep."

"I'm just not willing to pay it I guess," Molly said, her shoulders slumping.

"Maybe you're just smarter than the others. Kirsten could die trying to be popular. You could have died."

"I wasn't killing myself to be popular. I had no chance to be popular, not after what I let Lance do."

"That's the part you don't want to talk about, right?"

Molly nodded.

"Then I'm going to give you your next thinking exercise. I want you to make a list of all the people in your life that you used to consider your friend. You can include family members. I want you to list everyone who liked you, or who you liked."

"Why?"

"You'll find out at our next appointment. I'll be back tomorrow. The nurse will be here soon to take you for a shower."

CHAPTER 17

Dr. Karen sat down and smiled. "I'm sorry I'm early today, I had a scheduling conflict. How's your lunch?"

Molly was poking at the tray with a plastic fork. "I don't want it."

"I was told you didn't eat anything yesterday. They're talking about putting you back on the IV. Why aren't you eating?"

Molly shrugged. "The food isn't very good. And I haven't been eating much lately anyways."

"Why not?"

"I just wanted to lose weight. And don't worry; my mom already scolded me for missing meals. She was going to buy more fruit and sign me up for a gym instead."

"Both good ideas. I know hospital food isn't very good. Consider it a threat. If you don't get better you'll have to eat more of it."

Molly knew it was supposed to be a joke but she didn't smile, she just pushed the tray aside. "So what are we talking about today?"

"Did you make that list?"

"Yeah."

"How many people were on it?"

"Including people who now hate me? Thirteen. But I didn't count any teachers because they're not really friends."

"Sometimes they can be. But let's work with this list. Thirteen people. How many of them would you cross off that list?"

"Four for sure, I don't know if Brandon and I will still be friends when all this is done. My mom and step-dad should hate me but I don't think they do."

"I know they don't. So there are still nine people on that list. Did you know that my list is only twelve people long?"

"Really?"

"Yeah. Most people only have a dozen close friends and family members, or less. Does that mean we're all popular? Or does that mean we're all losers?"

Molly frowned. "What about all the people you work with? Aren't they your friends?"

"Not really. I know them to say hi to them or to eat lunch with them but I wouldn't go out for coffee with them or have them over for a BBQ. I don't know them well enough, or we don't have enough in common."

"But do they like you?"

"I don't know. I certainly don't like everyone who works here but I have to be polite to them because we work together."

"High school is different."

"Yes, I remember that. Teenagers can be very cruel to each other."

"Yeah, and ALL of them are being cruel to me, all at the same time."

"And that hurts, doesn't it?"

Molly nodded.

"It hurt you enough that you couldn't face it any more. I get that. Now you have a choice ahead of you. Are the nine people on your list enough for you? Do you still need to be popular with everybody or can you just be friends with those nine people, and a few others that may come and go in your life over the next few decades?"

"I don't know."

"Think about that. I won't see you now until Friday. You're not too bored, are you?"

"I'm bored to tears," Molly said. "But I'm going to eat my lunch now."

Karen smiled. "I'll see you Friday."

Joanna was on the phone again. Ever since Molly had been taken to the hospital the phone had been ringing off the hook. If she went to visit Molly, or went anywhere for that matter, she would come home to at least a dozen messages on the machine, so when she wasn't answering calls she was returning them. Friends and family called to see how Molly was doing. Hospital staff, police officers, and the school secretary called either to give updates or request more information. Newspaper and television reporters called for details they could publish or broadcast.

She finished reassuring her aunt that Molly was recovering and hung up the phone. When it didn't ring right away she made a mad dash for the bathroom. She even had time to find a cup of coffee before the next call came in. She answered it, trying to keep the weariness from her voice.

"I'm looking for Molly Waters," the male voice on the other end said.

"Who's calling please?"

"My name is Mr. Chang. I am the owner of Chang's Groceries."

Joanna sank to the couch. "What is your interest in my daughter?"

"Just over a week ago she came into the store. One of the stock boys caught her and two boys in the chip aisle and chased them all away. She dropped her basket and her money. At first I was hoping to find her because she broke a dozen eggs and they ruined the apples she had in her basket."

"Mr. Chang, I'm sorry about …"

"No, no, please hear me out. When I saw her on the news I was so happy. I want to give you the money back."

"Mr. Chang, that's very considerate of you, especially because there wasn't much there."

"Not much there? She had over a hundred dollars in her hand."

The truth hit Joanna like a fist to the stomach as she put Mr. Chang's words together with the date and time Molly must have been in that store. "Take out what you need to pay for the broken eggs and spoiled fruit. Donate the rest to charity."

"That is a lot of money. I'm sure Molly would want it returned to her."

"It's not Molly's money."

"The stock boy saw her drop it."

"Mr. Chang, those boys were trying to pay my daughter for sex against her will. Your stock boy is a hero; he stopped them from hurting a sixteen year old girl. If you don't want to give the money to charity, give it to him. And if you have any security footage of those boys, give it to Detective Price and tell him what you told me. I'll give you his contact information."

When Joanna hung up the phone she was shaking. *Oh Molly, I'm so sorry. You're mine to love, mine to keep, and I couldn't keep you safe. I sent you to that store. If only I had kept you home that day! I'm sorry.* Silent tears streamed down her face. The next time the phone rang, Joanna ignored it.

On Thursday Joanna brought Molly's backpack to the hospital. Instead of homework it contained two changes of clothes, a stack of novels, a Sudoku puzzle book, a crossword puzzle book, and half a dozen pencils. Even with the added distractions Molly was happy to see Dr. Karen Friday afternoon.

"You're looking better today," Karen said. "And the nurses are happy that you're eating again."

"You're right though, the food is terrible. What are we talking about today?"

"Oh, you're actually eager to start. Why's that?"

"Because I don't like reading, or number puzzles, or word puzzles and I'm bored."

"Then let's start. The other day we talked about popularity. Today we're going to talk about you."

Molly now felt less enthusiastic about the next half hour. "What about me?"

"Why did you cut your hair like that?"

"What's wrong with my hair?" Molly said, her hand going to her head.

"Nothing at all," Karen said, leaning back in her chair. "It's interesting that you got defensive about it. Why did you cut it that way?"

"I saw something similar in a magazine and I wanted to try it. It was purple to start with."

"Good. Do you wear make-up?"

"I didn't, not until I started dating Lance."

"When you get out of the hospital will you keep wearing make-up?"

"I think I will, yes."

"Because Lance liked it?"

Molly shook her head. "I like it. I like the way I look with big smoky eyes."

"Okay, what about jewelry. Do you wear any?"

Molly shook her head.

"What style clothes do you wear?"

This time Molly shrugged. "I don't have a style. I just sort of wear a little of whatever."

"So you wear whatever's main stream?"

"I guess so."

"Do you like the way you look?"

"No."

"What don't you like about you?"

"I'm fat. I like make-up but I know nothing about it and now Kirsten won't do it for me anymore so I'll end up looking dumb in it. I can't wear cool clothes because most of it doesn't look good on me because I'm fat. I wanted to dye my hair green this time. I'm tired of blue hair." She stopped. She hadn't meant to say that last part.

"Did you know you can change everything on that list?"

Molly and Dr. Karen worked together for another week. They talked more about popularity and self-image and they talked about new topics like Molly's family and hobbies. In that time Molly was moved from the general ward to the psychiatric observation ward. The room was smaller but more comfortable and Molly was allowed to walk around so long as she stayed in the ward.

Molly's mom came every day and Hank came with her when he could. Halfway through the week Brandon and Barb knocked on the door while Molly was staring at a crossword puzzle.

"Hide this," Barb said, handing Molly a box of chocolates. "I'm betting the hospital food isn't great. This should help fill the gaps."

Molly forced a smile and tried to give the box back. "The food is better now that I've been transferred."

"Then you can entertain your visitors with some," Barb replied. And then she went on talking about her job, the weather, the latest celebrity gossip, and seemingly anything else that crossed her mind. She laughed at her own comments and talked too loud, not caring that Molly wasn't responding.

Brandon hovered behind his mom looking embarrassed.

Finally Barb said, "But I'm going to get myself a coffee and leave you too to visit. I always enjoy talking with you Molly." She waved and disappeared.

Brandon sat in the vacated chair. "Sorry about her. That's how she deals with strong emotions."

"By talking?"

"Yeah. I think that's how she deals with everything since she never seems to stop."

"Are you going to talk?"

"I'm going to try."

"Have you come to tell me how much everyone at school misses me and how I should come back?"

Now Brandon hesitated. "No, I hadn't planned to talk about school."

"Are you jealous that everyone's paying attention to me?"

Another hesitation. "When we knew you were going to live the school made an announcement and said anyone who needed to speak to a councillor could. Some people did go talk. I know I did."

"And? How's everyone doing?"

"Uh, well, Kirsten is in trouble. Seems she's also in the hospital and everyone feels real bad for her."

"Oh."

"The teachers stop me in the halls and ask how you're doing. I tell them you're still recovering."

She swallowed hard. "Lance?"

"I haven't seen him around much."

"Of course."

"Actually I haven't spoken to any of your friends since the swimming pool. But Lance was expelled from school, probably because of the photos."

"Mr. Penner said they couldn't do anything about that because it didn't happen on school property."

"Oh," Brandon said. "Well, I'm sure he had his reasons."

Molly studied him for a moment. "You know what happened, don't you?"

"Of course not. I should go. I'll see you later."

"Don't bother coming back."

"I'm too stubborn to listen now, Molly. I'll see you later."

Later that day Detective Price came in to see Molly. She held out the box of chocolates. "Did you want one?"

"No, thank-you Molly."

She forced a smile and let the box drop back to the table. "Did you arrest Lance?"

"Yes, we did. He's been formally charged with five counts of distributing child pornography online, and we're still trying to determine how best to charge him for the text versions of the photos. He's also been charged with the solicitation of a minor."

"But we were dating. Won't that charge be dismissed because a boyfriend is allowed to say 'hey, wanna have sex?' to his girlfriend?"

"You're right, but we were given evidence that proves he bought you items with the intent of exchanging them for sex. It doesn't matter if you pay a person in cash, goods, or favours; if payment exchanges hands then we call it solicitation."

"Will I be charged?"

"No. He lied to you about his intentions until he had you alone."

"So will the photos finally come down?"

"They're down now, yes. That's really why I'm here. I want to apologize to you. My superior officer saw the photos and the comments and told us to leave it all online a little longer. He felt we could catch a few more predators through those comments. I agreed with him and we will be pressing charges against thirty-seven individuals for sexual harassment, and solicitation plus another four thousand people have been brought to the attention of national agencies, here and in the US, for the distribution of child pornography."

"Oh."

"Molly, no matter what good may have come from leaving those pictures up, I still messed up. I should have called you and warned you so that you could stay offline and away from those photos until this was all over. I should have told you what we were planning."

"It's okay."

Her deadpan voice told him otherwise. "Arrangements are being made for your testimony in court. No one will be present accept for the lawyer working the case, the defense lawyer, the judge, and any adult you feel you need to be present for your well-being."

"When will the trial be?"

"We don't know yet. Lance has his bail hearing today and his sentencing hearing in a week. They set the date for the trial at the sentencing hearing."

"Okay."

"Is there anyone else we should talk to, anyone who would testify about Lance's behaviour towards you?"

"No."

"Molly, there's one other thing. Lance has hurt a lot of girls in the last three years. We found a lot of pictures on his phone and hard drive. We're talking to as many of those girls as we can find and it sounds like he used the pictures to get sex from them."

"So I was just another nobody in his life."

"I'm sorry, that's not how I meant it. Because you stood up to him he can't hurt anyone else."

"Okay, sure. That's wonderful."

Now it was Detective Price who forced a smile. "I'm sorry you got hurt in all of this, Molly. I hope you feel better." He stood, catching his foot on the bedside table causing him to stumble back. He nodded to Molly and left.

Dr. Karen came in as Molly was finishing her breakfast Monday morning. "You're early again," Molly said, handing her empty tray to the nurse.

"I switched your appointment with someone else's today so that we would have longer together."

Molly frowned. "Why do we need more time today?"

"Because we're going to talk about your suicide attempt today."

Molly shook her head and got out of bed, walking to the window. "No. I don't want to."

"I know you don't. We'll go gently, okay? One step at a time, one question at a time, it won't be easy, but we need to do this."

"No."

"Molly, all week you've been skirting around certain subjects. You won't talk about Facebook. You won't talk about your fights with Lance. You won't talk about your last few days before the attempt. Bottling it up is dangerous. If we don't sort out why you attempted to kill yourself chances are you'll try again, no matter how good you feel right now."

"I'm fine. I don't want to talk about it. I don't want to think about it. I don't want to dig up the memories. I don't want to talk about the pictures!"

"Then let's talk about Lance. You fought with him twice. What were the fights about?"

"I already told you. He wanted sex. He says he paid for sex when he bought me nice things and that I was a prude for not giving it to him. Then he kicked me out. That was it."

"So there was nothing about the pictures in that first fight?"

"No."

"When were the pictures taken?"

"It doesn't matter."

"Was he expecting sex because of the pictures?"

"Maybe. I don't know. He never said so."

"Why did you let him take pictures of you?"

"I didn't let him!!!" Molly spun and started pacing the small space. "I didn't let him do anything! I didn't want him to kiss me or touch me. I didn't want him to take those pictures and I sure as hell didn't want him to share them with anybody. He just wouldn't listen. He never listened. No one ever listens to me!! They all wanted to change me. They all wanted to humiliate me or use me. None of them ever cared about me and now they've made sure that everyone else hates me too."

"What did they do, Molly?"

"They told lies about me."

"What lies?"

"It doesn't matter." Molly's burst of anger faded as quickly as it had risen. Now she paced back to the window and hugged herself. "No one can stop them. No one wants to stop them."

"Molly, what are they saying about you? What was so horrible that you wanted to die?"

Molly shook her head, slow and sad.

"Did they call you fat and ugly? Did they call you names? Did they insult your intelligence?"

"They called me a slut," Molly said.

Karen had expected her to turn and rage again. When the words came out small and emotionless instead they cut through her professional shell. Now, on the edge of tears, all she could do was listen as Molly told the window her darkest secrets in a voice that sometimes quivered but was otherwise void of emotion.

"They said I would have to whore myself out to be popular. Some of them said I was too ugly even for that. Lance said I was a slut, that I was calling him all the time for sex. Lance said I was kinky, that I wouldn't say no. He gave people my name, showed them pictures of me without my shirt on, and threatened to give them my home address.

"And I was stupid enough to walk right into it. Maybe I didn't let him take the first pictures but I believed him when he said they were private. I believed him enough that I sent him more. I thought that would make him love me again. But he never loved me in the first place. He never even cared, not even a little.

"When I found the pictures I tried to get Lance to take them down. He laughed in my face and called me names and threw me away. Literally. The bruise is healed now but it was there, right on my knee. My friends wouldn't help me but Julie was right in there with everyone else, making fun of me online. I wasn't important enough to help; I was only worth something if they could make fun of me.

"The school refused to help. They said it wasn't their problem. Only when my mom threatened them did they agree to look into it. But they wanted me to get the names of every boy who walked up to me and asked me to do dirty things.

"Have you ever had a complete stranger walk up to you and ask you for sex? Or a blow job? I had a complete stranger kiss me because he thought I was a whore. The school won't stop it. The cops can't stop it. My mom can't stop it. I can't go back, I can't face them. I hate people staring at me and this is worse."

"Your first overdose, where does it fit in to the story?"

"Right after the second fight with Lance. I called in sick to school the next day and Lance sent me a text message threatening to give his friends my address. He said they would keep me company. I was so scared that strange boys would show up at my door and hurt me and that no one could stop them."

"And your second overdose?"

"After the boys in the store kissed me."

"Why didn't you go through with it the first time?"

"I remembered something my mother said, about things you can take back, and things you can't take back. I wasn't ready to do something I couldn't take back, but after those boys cornered me ..." She shivered.

Karen sat in her chair and watched the broken sixteen-year-old across the room. She pulled her own emotions in tight, locking them back inside the box of professionalism. She took a deep breath. "Molly, I ..." She took another deep breath and tried again. "The adults at your school are idiots. There is so much more they could have done for you. Detective Price was here the other day, and he is making progress. Maybe it was stupid of him to use you as a lure to catch more people, especially without warning you, but they are doing something."

"Can they make people see me differently? Can they make the kids at my school stop whispering about me when I walk past them? Can they make me invisible again?"

"No."

"Can my school, or the police, or my mom, promise me that no one will corner me in the grocery store again?"

"No."

"I can't go back. I can't handle the fear and humiliation. If someone tries to touch me or kiss me I'll try again because it's the only way to stop them. They can't hurt me if I'm dead. And next time ..." She stopped, took a deep breath, and turned to look at Dr. Karen. "Next time there won't be a note."

Dr. Karen met Molly's stare until Molly finally turned back to the window. She took a few deep breaths then said, "I need something to drink. Did you want something? I can grab you a can from the machine in the staff room down the hall, if you'd like."

Molly shook her head.

When Dr. Karen came back Molly was perched on the edge of the bed, still staring out the window. She sat down next to her patient and took in the view. There wasn't much to see on this side of the hospital, just busy street and a grocery store across the way. People rushed about, trucks honked their horns, and no one paid any attention to the big grey building or the girl looking out the fifth story window.

"Even if Detective Price takes the pictures down, even if he puts Lance in jail, this won't stop. The teasing won't stop. They'll blame me for whatever happens to Lance. They'll never like me, they'll never accept me, and they'll never leave me alone."

"During one of our first meetings I asked you about the people who still like you, the ones who have stuck by you. Do you remember that?"

Molly nodded.

"Are those nine people worth living for? If those nine people like you, is that enough validation in your life? Can you face ridicule from the other students in your school if you have the love, acceptance, and support of those nine people?"

"I don't know. You don't know what it's like to have a stranger kiss you without asking."

"No, I don't. But I'm betting you were afraid. I bet you felt vulnerable, alone, and helpless."

"Worthless," Molly added. "Humiliated, terrified, lost, sick."

"It didn't occur to you to report them to someone?"

Molly shook her head. "No one wanted to help me. No one could help me. Everything I did to stop it was pointless. What's the use of trying anymore?"

CHAPTER 18

When Dr. Karen came in the next day she handed a paper to Molly.

"You're letting me out of here?" Molly asked, skimming the official document.

"Yes, I am. You'll be released tomorrow. I am recommending that you continue to see a psychologist once a week until he says you're no longer a high-risk teen. I also recommend that someone else go through your Facebook account and clear all the garbage off of it before you log back on."

"I don't want my mom to see my Facebook!"

"It's on the internet, Molly, it's not exactly private. You need to get rid of all the toxic elements in your life and focus on the positive. I don't think you're clinically depressed, I think this was a situational case and if you don't remove yourself from the situation you'll end up attempting again."

"Maybe that's what I want."

"You're a very contrary person, Molly. Agreeing with a grown-up doesn't make you foolish or weak. You don't have to argue with everyone just for the sake of arguing."

"So that's it? I don't have to see you again?"

"I thought that would make you happy?"

"Who's this other doctor I have to work with?"

"He's nice, about my age so you're not stuck with someone old and out of touch. He has teenage kids so he knows what's going on in the world that you're living in. I think you'll come to like him, eventually."

Molly was about to argue but she was tired of arguing and tired of having to come up with angry remarks so she just sighed and nodded.

"You've come a long way in these last few days. Don't let a few assholes stop you from recovering."

"Don't let my mom catch you saying that or she'll yell at you too." Molly didn't realize she'd made a joke until she saw Karen smiling. Molly smiled too.

"The doctors want you under observation for another day but I won't see you again. I have other patients to see now. You have some tough choices ahead of you, Molly, but you're stronger than you think." Karen smiled, nodded once, and left.

All Molly wanted to do when she got home from the hospital was hide in her room and go online but her mom and step-dad wanted to talk first. They all sat in the living room looking at each other as an awkward silence built around them.

Finally her mom said, "Molly, we've had meetings with Dr. Karen while you were in the hospital. I … we understand that things are going to be difficult for you and we want to help. If there's anything we can do …"

"I just need some time alone," Molly said. "I just want to be left alone. I don't want to pretend I'm okay just to make everybody happy. I'm not okay. I don't know when or if I will be okay."

Her mom nodded. "I have to keep going, Molly. I'm not trying to force you to go further or faster than you're willing to go, but I just have to be normal. I'll call you for dinner because I always call you for dinner, but if you aren't comfortable eating with us I'll understand."

"Your appointments with Dr. Jesse Mitchell are on Thursdays at 10am. I know it's early but it's the only regular slot he had open and we didn't want to wait to get you in to see him. Dr. Karen was pretty adamant about you seeing someone on a regular basis."

Molly nodded and forced a smile. "Right."

"You can talk to us anytime you want to, Molly. We will listen, no matter what."

"Of course Mom. Can I go lie down? I'm really tired."

"Yes. Of course. Go on. I'm sorry; we shouldn't be pestering you with all this right now." Her mom smiled. "Anything you need, honey, we're here for you."

Molly sat in front of her laptop staring at the black screen. Brandon had said so little about her friends during all his visits to the hospital that she didn't know what to expect. *Do they miss me? Did they even care that I was dying? Will they be happy to see me getting better?*

Molly turned the laptop on and waited. The seconds dragged by until she could start the internet and navigate to Facebook.

She had been ready to learn she'd been ignored. She'd been hoping that everyone had been cheering her on and sending her well-wishes. She'd completely forgotten that no one had touched her account since before the attempt.

The photos had finally been removed from Lance's account but with the photos gone people had turned on her directly. Lance's friends had all sent vicious, hateful messages blaming her for his expulsion from school and his run-in with the police.

She stared at the messages for a long time, tears welling up in her eyes. The police hadn't given her back her cellphone yet and everyone in the hospital had practically doted on her. Now she sat face-to-face with the brutal comments of her peers and wet hot tears of despair and self-loathing.

Blindly she began typing in the status box: *"Everyone thinks I'm a worthless human being. Doesn't anyone care that I lived?"*

It was the middle of the day, in the middle of the week, and Molly didn't expect any answer, let alone the sudden flood of answers.

"Great, you're out of the hospital."

"Of course we don't think you're worthless, god, can't you take a joke?"

"We were just teasing you Molly; I can't believe you believed us."

"Can't you take a joke? Lance was right, you are a prude."

"No one really wanted you to die so stop whining."

"You got Lance in some serious trouble over a stupid joke. Why would you do that?"

"Get over yourself, Molly. No one likes a whiner. Just laugh along with the joke, even if you're too dumb to get it."

"God, you're such a loser. How you could have taken us seriously?"

And on and on it went until Molly felt ashamed for ever bothering them. *"I'm sorry,"* she typed in the comments. *"I'm still really depressed."*

"You're not the only one with problems."

As if to prove the point Kirsten's status updated. *"I can't stop throwing up. My life is hell but at least I still want to live it – unlike some people who take the smallest excuse to do stupid shit just to make everyone feel sorry for them."*

Molly felt helpless, frozen by the words that continued to pour in over the afternoon. She sat staring at the screen, reading them all. When her mother called for supper she called back that she wasn't hungry, finally shut the computer off, and crawled into bed.

The next day wasn't any better. Or the next. Or the next. Everyone on Molly's friend list was concerned about Kirsten's eating disorder, but not one of them cared enough to reply to any of Molly's statues. And when they did reply it was to tell her to stop whining.

Molly didn't eat at all until her third day home. Her stomach was so empty she felt like she was going to throw up. She waited until she was sure everyone would be out of the kitchen and stumbled through the house. She grabbed an apple off the counter and shoved it in the front pouch of her sweater along with the last two buns from the bread box. She grabbed the half-finished bottle of pop from the fridge along with a bowl of grapes then turned to the cupboard and dug out a bag of chips.

She was ready to make good her escape when her mom came in, draining a cup of coffee as she walked. She looked startled to see Molly but quickly forced a smile. "Good morning. Are you going to sit and have breakfast?"

Molly shook her head and fled to her room. She spent the rest of her day eating and watching her news feed update with suicide memes and barbed comments.

Dr. Karen's description of Dr. Jesse had been accurate but Molly didn't find him reassuring or welcoming. She sat across the office from him with her arms crossed and her face set in a defiant scowl.

"Okay Molly, let's get started. I'm going to need some information about you."

"What kind of information?"

"Let's start with your internet habits. Before the attempt how many hours per week would you say you spent online for any reason: school work, entertainment, socializing, whatever?"

Molly shrugged. "An hour or two every day I guess. Why?"

"What about these last few days?"

"There's nothing else to do."

"So probably eight hours or so every day. What sites do you frequent?"

"Mostly Facebook."

"Do you have a lot of friends?"

"Sure, I guess."

Dr. Jesse nodded, making notes on a pad on his desk. "How do your friends feel about your suicide attempt and your current recovery?"

"They think I was being stupid, that I should be better already." She shrugged. "It's my own fault I'm messed up this way. I can't do anything right, not even committing suicide."

"Is that what they tell you?"

Another shrug. Any progress she had made with Dr. Karen had been eroded by the cruel and careless behaviour of her Facebook friends.

"How often do you leave your room?"

"Only to eat and pee," she said. "Why does any of this matter?"

"Because these are measurable signs of recovery or concern," Dr. Jesse explained. "I can ask you every week how you're feeling and you can say 'good' or 'not good' but in comparison to what? To how you felt before the attempt? To how you felt in the hospital?"

"But I can lie about any of it."

"Of course you can. But why bother? I'm not asking intrusive questions about your feelings. I'm just collecting stats on your daily habits. Harmless."

"And nosy," she shot back. "I don't want to be here."

Dr. Jesse just smiled and continued asking questions. He took Molly's argumentative attitude in stride, meeting her insults and complaints with pleasant explanations and calm counter-arguments.

As Molly was leaving Dr. Jesse said, "I'd like you to try to leave your room more. I don't care if you wait until everyone's asleep and go dance in the living room in the dark, but you need to let yourself out of that box more often, and for longer periods. I know it feels safe right now, but there's a lot more to the world than your bedroom and a laptop."

"Sure, whatever," Molly said and stalked out.

Molly sat in the passenger seat staring at all the people on the sidewalks and the buildings behind them. Her mother sighed and said, "You know, Molly, Shannon's school play is coming up this weekend."

"So?"

"Molly, I said I wouldn't push, but it would mean a lot if you came to see her. She misses you, she's been worried about you, she …"

"She hates me and I deserve it. I don't want to ruin her play by showing up."

"Molly, I know a lot of harsh words were said, but she doesn't hate you. Will you at least think about it? Please?"

Knowing there was only one way to get out of the conversation she said, "Fine, I'll think about it," and went back to staring at the strangers outside her window.

Molly was staring at a picture on Facebook while thoughts chased each other through her mind. The picture was a simple sunset over water in vivid oranges and reds but it was the text printed across the picture that had captivated Molly.

"How do people make it through life without a sister?"

The picture hadn't been posted by Shannon, it hadn't even been directed at her, but the words stared back at her, both questioning and accusing. Guilt and sorrow that had been buried for weeks beneath layers of anger and defiance welled up inside her.

She had seen the pain in Shannon's eyes every time she had lashed out at the younger girl. She hadn't wanted to feel sorry for her sister, didn't want to feel sorry now, but she knew she had messed up, and she knew she had lashed out at Shannon for no reason.

Why that image had crossed her news feed on that day and why she had singled it out from all the other dark depressing images she didn't know. But she did know that she couldn't bury the pain or the guilt again. *And I sure as hell can't live with it.*

That evening she slipped from her room and went downstairs. Her mom often worked late on her design contracts and Molly found her staring intently at a zoomed in section of something red on her computer screen.

"I'll go," Molly said softly from the office doorway.

Her mom jumped and spun around. "It's you. You startled me. I didn't realize you were still up."

"I'll go to the play this weekend."

"That's wonderful, honey." Her mom smiled and Molly could see the relief in her eyes.

"Good night." She turned and trudged back upstairs, too tired to even return the smile.

Molly got dressed and brushed her hair without looking in the mirror. The hair on the left needed to be shaved again and the blue was faded and noticeably growing out. She pulled a hooded sweater on over her outfit and pulled the hood over her head. She found her sneakers under a pile of laundry and pulled them on. She took half a dozen deep breaths and stepped out of her room. Her mom was waiting in the living room and smiled when she came in.

"I'm ready," Molly said, forcing a smile.

"Thank-you for doing this," her mom said, laying a hand on her arm.

Her step-dad was waiting in the car. Once Molly and her mom were buckled in he backed down the driveway.

"Does Shannon know I'm coming?"

"No," her mom said. "We didn't want to put any pressure on you. I know you're having a hard time just leaving your room, and I don't blame you for that one bit."

"You didn't say, 'I understand'," Molly said.

"That's because I don't," her mom replied. "I've never been where you are now, Molly. I won't insult what you're feeling by telling you I understand it. But I'll support you while you try to sort it all out."

"Thanks." She turned her attention to the trees going by her window. Trees were safer than people.

Molly and her mom sat in the back corner of the theatre but even there Molly felt like everyone who walked past was staring at her with pity or curiosity. Her step-dad took a seat closer to the front so he could take some pictures during the show.

The play was maybe an hour long, including intermission, and Molly could feel the anxiety building the entire time. Her heart pounded as her chest got tighter. Her throat always felt dry. She couldn't keep her eyes on the stage; she had to keep checking to make sure no one she knew could see her.

And then Shannon walked out on the stage and started delivering her lines. Molly couldn't take her eyes off her younger sister. *Where's the timid little thing that's been sulking around the house? Who is this girl with the big voice and the big smile? Did she really memorize all those lines?*

As soon as the play was over Molly retreated to the car to wait. Shannon had to stay at school for a pizza dinner and then the evening performance. After congratulating her Molly's mom and step-dad came out to the car. The entire way home Molly stared out the window, lost in thoughtful silence.

At home she opened her laptop, ignoring the internet for the first time since getting out of the hospital, and opened a blank document. Taking a deep breath she began to type.

"Shannon, I went to see your play this afternoon. You were amazing. You lit up the stage. You never forgot a line. I loved every minute you were on stage.

"I know I said some unforgivable things about you, and to you. I know I was mean to you. I know there are no excuses for how I acted. It was easier to hate you then feel guilty about hurting you. It was easier to blame you than to blame myself.

"You're annoying sometimes, you really are. And sometimes I get angry at you. But today I was proud of you. Molly."

Molly stared at the screen for a long time and then hit the print button. There was only one printer in the house and she ran to the office downstairs to catch the paper before anyone else read it. She folded it carefully and slid it under Shannon's door.

When Shannon finally got home Molly was already curled up in bed pretending to sleep. She had spent the evening on the computer scrolling through pages of dark, depressing images, and her own status updates with no replies. She felt alone and bundling up under the blankets helped her build an illusion of security.

"I just want to die," she whispered. "No one sees me."

Her door burst open pouring light across the floor. A small figure danced in and bounded up on the bed. Molly was so startled by Shannon's appearance and her hug that she found herself hugging Shannon back.

"I knew you didn't hate me," Shannon whispered. "And I don't hate you either. I don't care if you think you're broken, you're still the best big sister in the world."

Molly blinked back tears. "Thanks," she whispered back.

"Good night Molly."

"Good night Shannon."

CHAPTER 19

Molly was sifting through her news feed hitting and like on pictures of pill bottles with suicidal messages and 'I hate myself' memes. Her status update read, "The only person in the world who cares about me is my little sister." There were no replies on it, or her last three status updates.

She scrolled down and saw the picture of Lance and Julie. He had his arms around her and she was obviously holding her phone up to take the photo. Under it was an almost identical picture but in this one he was kissing her cheek. Tears crawled down Molly's face.

She was scrolling through Lance's photos looking for anything of the two of them together when Brandon came in. He dropped a burnt disc on the desk and sat on the edge of the bed behind her.

She frantically wiped the tears away. "You can't just barge in here."

"I was sent to check on you, and see if you wanted lunch."

"I don't! Now get out."

"What are you looking at?" He peered over her shoulder.

"Nothing, okay? Get lost."

"Why are you looking at Lance's page?"

"I said get lost!" Molly clicked back to her news feed.

"What are all those pictures doing there? Did you post those?"

"No, I didn't, not all of them. I didn't even share most of them. Why do you care?"

"I don't think staring at pictures of pills and scribbled notes and depressing quotes is going to make you feel better."

"Maybe I don't want to feel better."

"Does it make you feel good to be contrary? You argue with everything I say."

"I don't have to agree with you on anything. I don't even want you here."

"Molly, can't you see what they're doing to you? Look back at their profiles and their posting history. I'm betting that not one of those people started posting the depressing suicidal memes until after you reported Lance to the police."

"Are you saying I make people depressed?"

"No, I'm saying they're trying to make you depressed."

"Why would they do that? They're my friends. They care about me."

"Your mom cares about you; she calls my mom crying all the time because she's so worried about you. Your step-dad cares about you; he missed work to see you in the hospital. Your sister cares about you, she just wants you to smile at her and she'd be happy! Did you know your cousin Stephanie has called every day since the attempt to see how you're doing?"

"If my cousin cares so much why didn't she come see me in the hospital?"

"Molly, she's attending college halfway across the country. She can't drop everything to be here and you know it. And if you want to play it that way, where were all your friends? Why didn't they come visit you in the hospital? Why didn't they send you cards or flowers or chocolates? Why are they still trying to hurt you instead of trying to help you heal?"

"You don't know anything about it!"

"I know more than you think I do. I know more than you do. You need to wake up, Molly; before you spiral down so low you try again. And don't give me that crap about wanting to die because I don't believe it. I believe you can beat this but you need to get rid of the toxic people in your life. You need to make a decision to get better no matter what the cost."

Tears streamed down Molly's cheeks. "Get out. I don't want you in here. I don't want you sticking your nose in my business. I didn't ask you to come in here and lecture me! Get out!"

"Fine, just hate me for giving a damn about what happens to you." Brandon stormed out of the room.

Molly sat shaking in her seat. A notification popped up on her screen with its customary 'bing' but she didn't turn to look. Her chest felt hollow and the pounding of her heart echoed off her ribs until the sound filled her ears and made her head feel heavy.

Through the pounding she heard the back door slam and she shut her eyes as the guilt settled like a rock in her gut. A moment later there was a knock at her door and her mom said, "Is everything okay?"

"Fine," she said. "I'm fine."

She waited until she heard her mother walking away and then opened her eyes again. By chance they settled on the clear plastic case sitting on top of a pile of laundry on her desk. She took it in her hand and stared at the hand-written label on the disc.

"Social Issues Presentation."

Her stomach knotted. She hadn't thought about the project in weeks. Her hands shook as she opened the case and put the disc in the player. Her media player popped open and she made the image full-screen.

At first the camera bounced around, showing Brandon at the front of the room setting up his presentation board and organizing his paper. The camera quickly steadied and she heard the teacher's voice ask, "Are you ready Brandon?"

"Yes, I'm ready."

"Okay," the teacher said. "Our final presentation is Brandon. Please give him your full attention."

Brandon stood in front of a blank presentation board. Someone close to the camera snickered. Brandon took a deep breath and said, "I was going to do a presentation on drug usage but after recent events I changed my mind. I want to talk about teen suicide.

"Suicide is the second leading cause of death for youth between the ages of 10 and 24. People commit suicide for a variety of reasons."

Molly sat staring at the screen as Brandon went on about factors and statistics and warning signs. Throughout his speech his presentation board remained blank.

"Bullying is also a prominent motivator behind teen suicides. Weight, appearances, race, sexuality, and odd or misunderstood hobbies or interests have all made teens targets for bullies. In the last ten years bullying has moved out of the hallways, change rooms, and cafeterias and into the digital world. Teens are teased via text message and over social media. Hate pages are put up online and receive thousands of hits every day. This form of bullying goes unchecked because schools cannot supervise or intervene and freedom of speech on the internet is often twisted to include bullying. Add to that a bully's favourite defense 'it was just a joke' and it's no wonder authorities are powerless to stop it.

"I would like to look at three cases where cyber bullying drove a teenager to suicide. In doing so I would like to show that this behaviour is not funny and should never be dismissed as a joke."

Finally Brandon half turned and stuck two pieces of paper to the board. Two teenage girls now smiled out at the class. "These girls are Amanda Todd and Megan Meier. They both committed suicide. Megan killed herself in 2006 after two fellow students, and a parent, created a fake MySpace account and befriended her online. After weeks of very pleasant exchanges this fake friend changed his tone and told Megan: "Everybody in O'Fallon knows who you are. You are a bad person and everybody hates you. Have a shitty rest of your life. The world would be a better place without you." She hung herself that same day.

"Amanda was coaxed into revealing her body to an online friend. He then blackmailed her and tormented her online for three years. Using fake accounts on social media sites he turned everyone at her school against her. When she changed schools, and towns, he did it again. After three years of this continual abuse she killed herself."

Molly was speechless; the class in the foreground of the video was not. There were murmurs and whispers until the teacher finally said, "That's enough. Let's let Brandon finish his presentation."

Brandon placed a third photo on the presentation board. "This is Molly. She was in our class. Now she's in the hospital. She attempted suicide, not because of a mental illness or a learning disorder, or because she used drugs. Like Amanda Todd and Megan Meier, she was pushed into suicide."

The class erupted and the camera started shaking again. Over the talking and shouting of the students the teacher was saying, "Sit down, all of you. Sit down! Be quiet, please, and listen to the end of the presentation. Shut up and sit down or I'll fail the whole class!"

Order was slow to return and the camera stabilized again.

"I'm not making this up," Brandon said. "I'm not pointing fingers but I'm not making this up. I know most of you have heard some version of what happened but I am going to fill you in on the actual events. Molly's boyfriend, Lance Maher, got angry when Molly refused to have sex with him. He left her to walk home, alone, in the small hours of the morning. He then posted topless photos of Molly online and shared them with his friends via text message. And just so you're aware, the photos have been taken down. Possession or sharing of those images is considered owning or distributing child pornography and you can be arrested.

"So, Lance posts pictures which Molly believed would remain private. And when she confronted him he insulted her and physically abused her – on school property. He blamed Molly."

There were more mumbles from the crowd and someone even said, "It was her fault."

"He posted a lie online, portraying Molly as, please excuse me language, as a slut. Because of the pictures and Lance's comments Molly was subjected to sexual harassment from strangers, including two boys trying to force her to have sex with them.

"Molly attempted suicide in the face of these events. Most of you looked offended and horrified at the stories of Amanda Todd and Megan Meier. But of the eighteen people in this class twelve of them posted rude, insulting, or suggestive comments on the photos Lance posted. Twelve of you, at least, helped push Molly to suicide."

Chaos reigned. People stood from their chairs and shouted at Brandon. The camera shook and for a while pointed directly at the floor.

Molly held her breath as muddled noises poured from the speakers. Finally the noise quieted and the camera was righted.

Brandon took a deep breath before continuing. "In summary: bullying isn't a joke, we can't dismiss it. It is normal, ordinary teens who are the bullies, and the victims. Teens need to be held accountable for their words and actions, in school, on the streets, and online. If we are not, more of us will commit suicide. Are there any questions?"

"How can you prove any of that?"

"The cases of Amanda Todd and Megan Meier are public record. As for Molly, I have only told you what I witnessed myself or was able to confirm with her parents or the detective investigating the photos."

"Are the cops really charging people?" This voice sounded panicked.

"Yes, for sexual harassment, soliciting a minor, and spreading child pornography."

"What does soliciting mean?"

From behind the camera the teacher's voice said, "Asking someone for something, in this case, sex."

"You couldn't have known why Lance was expelled," said a male voice.

"I do, actually. I witnessed the fight in the hallway and turned a video of it over to Mr. Penner."

This uproar was smaller, mainly from the boys in the class, and it sounded like they were all demanding why Brandon would do such a horrible thing to such a cool person.

"All right," the teacher roared. "Everyone is going to sit down. Brandon's presentation is over; I'm putting an end to the questions. Sit down and …"

The video cut out.

It was after midnight. The house was silent except for the hums and bumps that all houses make and the soft whir of a computer fan. Molly sat in the same chair staring at her computer screen. She had watched Brandon's presentation a second time but the dismay at seeing her face on the board and the shock at hearing the last few weeks of her life walked through event-by-event had lessened.

Now she sat staring at her friend list on Facebook. Four hundred and seventy-two friends. It was the highest that number had ever been.

Her chest felt heavy. She couldn't take her eyes off the screen.

Four hundred and seventy-two people who say they are my friends. But how many of them came to see me in the hospital? How many of them helped Lance hurt me? How many of them really care about me?

She was terrified. She swallowed hard but still couldn't move.

If I delete them there's no going back. They won't re-friend me. If I just leave it maybe the depressing pictures will stop. Maybe I can be popular without Lance.

For the last several hours she had been wavering between this desperate hope and a stilling sense of clarity. The realizations that came in those moments scared her. She didn't want to be wrong about everything. She didn't want to feel this isolated anymore but she didn't know if keeping all her online friends would make the feeling better or worse.

I wish tomorrow was my appointment with Dr. Jesse. I need help. I need someone to talk to. I need someone to tell me what I'm supposed to do.

With that thought several things fell into place in her mind.

First was Dr. Karen saying, *"That's what this all comes down to, Molly. No matter what other people think, you have to love you enough to want to be in this world. You have to love you enough to see your strengths and your value even in the face of failure."*

Second was Brandon earlier that evening: *"I'm saying they're trying to make you depressed ... where were all your friends? Why didn't they come visit you in the hospital? Why didn't they send you cards or flowers or chocolates? Why are they still trying to hurt you instead of trying to help you heal?"*

Third was Lance, not a specific memory, just the way he said, *"Come here,"* all the time, or *"Drink the beer"*, or *"Get the hell out,"* like he could command her obedience simply because he was her boyfriend.

And that's what he was doing – commanding me. Do I really need someone to tell me what to do and who to be? It didn't work out too great last time. Taking a deep breath Molly reached for the mouse.

At first Brandon thought his alarm was going off. He fumbled for his phone and noticed two things simultaneously. It was 1am and Molly's name was on the screen of his phone. He panicked, now fully awake, and answered the call.

"Molly, is everything all right?"

"I feel alone," she said and he could hear the tears in her voice.

"You're not alone," he said. "I'm here. What happened?"

"I deleted them. There's no one to talk to."

"There's me, even if I am just a dweeb," Brandon said. "You didn't delete me, did you?"

She sniffled. "No."

"Or your cousins?"

"No."

"You're not alone."

"All the pictures and posts just disappeared. My news feed is empty!"

"There's more to life than a news-feed, Molly. Why don't I take you out for lunch tomorrow?"

"No! No, I can't. What if I run into someone I just deleted?"

"Ignore them."

"What if they talk to me? What if they're angry? What if …"

"Molly, I'll be right there with you. I'll chase them off if I have to. I'll even bring a big stick so they know I mean business."

She hiccupped and he knew she was trying to stay miserable. He also knew he had succeeded in making her smile if only for a moment.

"You deserve positive people in your life," he went on. "All the negative people should leave you alone."

"I don't know."

"Well, I'll come over at least and keep you company."

There were more sniffles and then, "Oh god Brandon, look at the time! Why did you even pick up the phone?"

"I was scared."

"I'm sorry. I shouldn't have called. I'm such a bother."

"Molly, thank-you for calling. Thank-you for trusting me."

"You're not mad?"

"No."

"I'm sorry. I should let you get some sleep. I should try to sleep. I …"

"I'll see you tomorrow Molly."

"Right."

"Good-night Molly."

"Good-night Brandon."

CHAPTER 20

Molly got dressed slowly. She didn't really want to go to the mall and face the world but everyone in her life felt she needed to get out of her room more. Even promising to eat three meals per day in the kitchen at meal times didn't win her any supporters.

She brushed her hair, checking a mirror of the first time in days. There was an inch of black roots on the long side and the shaved side looked messy. Her mom had already offered to help her with it but she had declined. Now she frowned at her reflection.

A knock on her door interrupted. "Molly? I'm on my way out. Do you need anything?"

Molly opened the door and said, "I want to cut my hair. I don't want to be that girl in the pictures."

"Done," Joanna said, reaching into her purse. "Here's the twenty I owe you for May, and the twenty for June. I'll see you for supper."

Molly stared at the money in her hand, only barely remembering to call, "Yeah. Thanks Mom," before her mom disappeared. Now alone in the house Molly went back to getting ready.

Brandon was already five minutes late when the phone rang. She'd gotten a new cellphone and had given the number only to family and to Brandon and Barb because so many people were calling and texting her to harass her. No one ever called for her on the land line so she didn't even think before picking it up.

"Hello?"

"Is that you Molly?"

Molly froze. "Who is this?"

"You little whore! Why the hell did you delete me from Facebook?"

"Lance? We're not …"

"You can't get rid of me, Bitch. This isn't over. You owe me for everything I bought for you and until I collect we're not finished."

The dial tone was music to Molly's ears.

Her hand shook as she hung up the phone and she turned to find Brandon letting himself in the side door. "Sorry I'm late. I had to drop my mom off and … Molly, what happened?"

"Nothing."

"You look like you saw a ghost."

"It's nothing, just an angry phone call."

"From who?"

"They never said," Molly lied. "Come on. I want to get my hair cut before lunch. I look horrible."

"You are looking a little scruffy around the edges," he said, nodding.

"Gee, thanks."

"You said it first! I was agreeing with you!"

She locked up and they bickered all the way to the car and Molly quickly forgot about the phone call.

They stopped at a little hair salon where, to Brandon's surprise, Molly had her hair chopped down to an all-around short, pixie style. That she dyed it neon green didn't surprise him. As they walked back out to the car he said, "I still think you should have gone with pink."

"No. I wanted to dye it green."

Molly and Brandon were sitting in the food court eating lunch when they were joined by a group of girls Molly barely recognized. Even if she couldn't place their names to their faces, they definitely knew all about her.

"Hi, Molly," said the first, a girl with pin straight brown hair. "What a pleasure to see you again."

The other girls snickered.

"You're looking so good now. I'd heard rumours that you'd lost weight. I guess trying to be popular is a hard habit to break. It's too bad losing weight won't help you."

Molly wanted to cry but not as badly as she wanted to run away.

"No one likes you anymore," said another girl.

"If you don't like her then why are you here talking to her?" Brandon snapped. "For fuck's sake, can't you pathetic vultures find something more productive to do than harass someone who just wants to be left alone?"

They stared at Brandon, shock written over every single one of their faces. "Well, if it isn't a dork in shining armour," the first girl said with a bitter smile. "You'd better watch yourself; Lance doesn't like it when people play with his girl."

"She's not 'his girl'," Brandon snarled. "Piss off already, you're ruining my lunch."

"Be seeing you, Molly." They called as they sauntered off.

One even wiggled her fingers in a wave and said, "I love your hair, troll snot green is so your colour."

"Let's go," Molly said, pushing her food away. "Let's get out of here. I can't do this."

"If that's what you want," Brandon said with a shrug. "I thought we could wander down to the music store. I need a gift for my mom's birthday."

"I can't, Brandon, please."

"Molly, you're doing really well."

"No, you're doing really well. You knew just what to say to those girls. I didn't know what to say. I would have run. I want to run now!"

"Then we'll run. But we'll run in the direction of the music store. Just a quick stop, I promise. If I don't get my mom a new CD I'll go crazy. She plays the same ones over and over again until I'm ready to take steel wool to the back of them."

"Brandon ..."

He finished packing up the leftover food. "Come on then, we'll get going."

After the stop at the music store they headed for the bathroom at Molly's insistence. Brandon leaned against the wall opposite the washrooms, pulled out the application he'd picked up at the music store, and ignored the comings and goings around him.

To Brandon's left someone snarled, "You're in deep shit, dweeb!"

The shove sent Brandon stumbling and it was luck more than talent or grace that saved him from landing on his ass. He tucked the papers away as he straightened.

"Go away Lance."

"Is that the best you can come up with?"

"No, but I'm not wasting time or effort thinking of insults or comebacks to waste on you."

"But you'll waste your time getting me expelled? Yeah, I know that was you. And you're wasting your time on that piece of shit, Molly. Or are you trying to be the hero? Help her through the rough stuff? Pick her up on the rebound? You were always jealous of me and her and now you're trying to be the knight in shining armour so you can get into her pants."

"Molly and I have been friends for sixteen years. I'm not giving up on her just because you tell me to. And I'm not helping her to get into her pants."

"You think I believe you?"

"I don't care what you think. You made it very clear you wanted nothing to do with her so why do you care if I hang out with her?"

"I broke up with her but that doesn't mean I'm done with her."

"Okay Brandon, let's ..." Molly stopped in the bathroom doorway.

Lance pointed at Brandon. "You just think about what I said." His glare turned to a sneer as his gaze swept over Molly and then he stalked away.

"Was he looking for me?" Molly whispered.

"No. Chance encounter. Come on, there's no point in hanging around here."

Brandon's first shift at the music store was a closing shift later that week. *At least the days are long and I don't have to walk to the bus in the dark,* he thought as he slipped out the staff exit at the back of the mall and into the warm night air. *This will be a lot worse come winter.*

As he walked around to the bust stop he considered walking all the way home. A familiar figure stepped out from behind the bus shelter and Brandon's mood darkened. *I guess I'm not going anywhere until a bus, and more importantly a bus driver, show up.*

"You don't listen, do you?"

"Cut the ominous stalker crap, Lance. If I call Detective Price he'll add intimidating a witness to you list of charges."

"You and Molly are both cowards, hiding behind the police. You need to stay away from Molly; she's mine, bought and paid for."

"She's a human. You can't buy people."

Lance was about to say more when the bus pulled up. Brandon boarded without a backward glance. As soon as the bus pulled away, without Lance, he pulled out his phone and dialed Molly's new cell number.

"Hello!"

"Hey Molly."

"How was work?"

"Not a lot of customers but there's a lot to learn. Look, Lance was waiting for me at the bus shelter. Has he been bothering you lately?"

"Not since we ran into him at the mall on Sunday. What did he want?"

"Be careful Molly. He thinks he owns you."

"Can you pick me up tomorrow?"

He could hear grim determination in her voice. "I can, but it has to be in the morning. I work after lunch."

"Fine, but come as early as you can. I have to see Dr. Jesse at ten and I want to do this first."

Brandon was surprised to see Molly waiting on her front step with a large shopping bag when he pulled up. "You really meant early," he said as she climbed in. "Where are we going?"

Molly gave him the address and directions.

Brandon put the car in gear and pulled away from the curb. "So, what's there?"

"Lance's house."

"Lance? Are you stupid? Should you be going anywhere near him?"

"I have to, Brandon."

"Didn't I tell you last night to be careful?"

"Didn't you tell me last night that he thinks he owns me?"

"And going there is going to prove what, exactly?"

"That he doesn't."

When Brandon pulled up in front of the unimposing bungalow with the neatly tended flower beds he turned off the car and opened his door.

"No." Molly said. "I have to do this on my own. Without you."

Brandon nodded and closed the door again. "If it takes too long I'm coming after you."

"We're not in a horror movie, Brandon," she said and got out of the car.

"Yes we are," he whispered as he watched her jog up the driveway, bag in hand.

To everyone else Molly looked determined, single-minded, and strong. Inside Molly was shaking with terror and now that she was alone on Lance's side step that terror was seeping through her brave façade.

She knocked again and took several deep breaths trying to slow her racing heart and steady her shaking hands.

Why didn't I let Brandon come with me? I could have made him promise to keep his mouth shut while I dealt with this. Why did I want to come here? This is dumb. He'll never listen.

Before she could talk herself around to running back to the car the door opened and all that separated Molly from Lance was a screen door.

He stared at her for a moment and then sneered. "Did you come back to pay up?"

"No. I came back to return something to you."

The sneer dropped from his face and his eyes narrowed. "Return what?"

The closed screen door gave her courage and she dropped the bag on the step at her feet. "Clothes, make-up, and lingerie. Everything you bought me is right here. And since I'm not in possession of it any more I don't owe you anything."

"I bought you food. I paid the taxes when you didn't have enough money."

"And I threw that shirt in the bag too. That's twenty dollars you owe me for the shirt. Keep the shirt and the twenty and call it even."

She stepped down onto the walkway.

"What am I supposed to do with a bag of clothes?"

"I don't care," she said without turning around.

She forced herself to walk down the driveway when everything inside her was screaming at her to run before he came after her. She got into the car and did up her seat belt. "Let's go," she said.

Brandon shook his head. "Well, at least you'll have something to talk to Dr. Jesse about."

As June gave way to July and July continued its steady march towards August Molly began spending more time in the living room and back yard, either with her mom, or Shannon, or Brandon. Her Facebook news feed was a lonely, boring place now that she was left with only Brandon and her cousins for friends and staring at the same screen for hours on end only made her feel more isolated. Dr. Jesse and Brandon had both been pushing her to get out of her room and she wasn't sure if she was tired of their nagging or just tired of being alone.

She ate lunch and supper with her family, when she was home. Brandon liked to go out, a lot, to the playground, or the shopping mall, or even just for a walk around town. The shopping mall was the hardest for Molly because that's where everyone went to hang out. Brandon was busy with work but sometimes Molly and Joanna would stop in and see him at the music shop.

Most days Molly felt like she was getting better, but any time she ran into someone from her school they teased and belittled until Molly was in tears and she spent hours locked in her room again. After every run-in her family was back to square one, coaxing her out or her room, coaxing her out of the house, until they started to worry that Molly would never really get better.

Molly stood at the backdoor staring at the doorknob. She took a few deep breaths. "It's just to the corner store to get milk," she said aloud to the empty house. "Mom will be really happy if I go get milk while she's at the dentist with Shannon. She'll be happy that I'm getting better. I can't always rely on Brandon to go with me everywhere and everyone gets so upset every time I give up and hide. I have to show them that I'm getting better so they'll stop being disappointed. Dr. Jesse says I need to be my own strength. I can do this."

She took a few more deep breaths, this time with her eyes closed. She took the first step before opening her eyes. Nothing bad happened so she took another, and another. Once out on the stoop she squinted and blinked and tried to keep her breathing even. She triple checked that the door was lock and double checked that she had her keys and her phone.

She stared straight ahead; fearful she'd catch the attention of some well-meaning neighbour on the four-block trip and walked purposefully down the sidewalk.

She breathed a sigh of relief as she rounded the corner and the store came into view. She crossed to the store and slipped inside, heading straight to the coolers in the back. The bell above the door jangled and Molly heard two people, a guy and a girl, talking and laughing. She grabbed the jug of milk and hurried to the cash register. From behind the two teens at the slushee machine could have been anyone but as her milk beeped through the scanner the girl turned – and smiled sharply at Molly.

"Hi Molly," Julie said, her smile growing.

For the first time in as long as Molly could remember Julie's smile didn't have that barbed look to it. *She looks happy to see me, almost too happy.*

And then the boy beside her turned and Molly's heart started pounding.

"I didn't think I'd see you again. In all the commotion from my expulsion and arrest and our little misunderstanding about property I forgot to tell you how surprised I was to hear you were in the hospital. I knew you were a failure but I didn't think you'd fail at committing suicide."

Molly could feel tears springing to her eyes. She didn't want to cry, not here, not in front of them, but there were so many tears.

Lance sneered at her, grabbed his drink, and said, "I'm going to get a snack."

"I'll be right there," Julie said.

"That'll be six dollars," the man at the cash register prompted.

Molly fumbled for her money and then fumbled with the change.

Julie said, "I used to think you were so lucky to have a boyfriend like Lance."

Molly stopped; her jug of milk already tucked in the crook of her arm, and really looked at the girl who had once claimed to be her friend. There were shadows around Julie's eyes that her make-up didn't quite hide and shadows on her arms. Worse was the haunted look in her eyes.

Lance came back with his snacks. "Julie, why are you still talking to her?"

"I was just telling her that Kirsten is finally out of the hospital."

"Who gives a damn about Kirsten? And why would you care if Molly's up on the latest gossip. Molly should be dead!"

Molly couldn't think about Julie's troubles anymore and she couldn't help. She ran the entire way home, pausing only when her grip on the milk jug started to slip. She set the milk down on the stoop and fumbled with her keys, dropping them twice before getting them into the lock. Just as they slid in the door opened and her mom stood in the doorway.

She reached out and drew Molly into a hug. "I was so worried about you."

Molly was stunned. "I thought I'd be back before you."

"Where were you?"

"I just went to the corner store for milk." She stepped free of her mom and retrieved the milk.

Her mom breathed a sigh of relief. "You've gone out so rarely and only with me or Brandon, that I wasn't expecting this. I'm proud of you for stepping outside your comfort zone like this."

"You're not mad that I scared you?"

"Of course not," her mom said, shaking her head. "Could you leave a note next time?"

"Yeah," Molly nodded. She handed her the milk. "I need to hide again. I just … I think it was too much too soon."

"Go right ahead. I'll call when supper's ready."

Molly fled.

Molly cried until her chest hurt and she had trouble breathing. As the sobs subsided she crawled off her bed and opened the desk drawer. From deep inside under a pile of old papers she pulled out the disposable razor. It belonged to her step-dad and she had stolen it the day after she'd gotten out of the hospital.

Just for emergencies, she had told herself. *Just in case I can't do this after all.*

Now she carefully pulled the razor apart, discarding the handle and the plastic frame, leaving only three neat, narrow blades. These she stared at for a long time.

"I knew you were a failure but I didn't expect you to fail at that."

She gingerly picked up one of the blades between thumb and forefinger and laid it against her wrist. She took a deep breath, held it, and pressed down, sliding the blade along her skin. The blood welled up, bright and warm and she bit her lip as she switched the blade to her other hand. This hand was shaking already and the blade slipped and bit deep.

She dropped the blade and clamped her hand over her wrist. She hadn't expected it to hurt so much. She cast about, her eyes settling on an old t-shirt which she wrapped around her arm. She opened her door a crack and peered out for a long time before dashing for the bathroom. She turned on the shower to hide the sounds of her rummaging through the medicine cabinet. She washed her arm and bandaged it then soaked the t-shirt. Most of the blood rinsed out and she was grateful she now had to do her own laundry.

Maybe a good soak and some laundry spray will get it clean enough.

She turned off the shower and bolted for her room again. In a frenzy she hid the blades and the broken handle. Behind her there was a knock at the door.

"Was that you in the shower?" her mom asked.

Molly almost said yes then realized her hair was still dry. "Uh, I was going to hop through the shower but I changed my mind. I didn't know how close supper was."

"It's ready."

"Okay, I'll be out in a second."

She grabbed her favourite hooded sweater and threw it over her head before stepping out into the hallway.

Her mom's forehead creased. "It's boiling outside," she said.

"Oh, yeah, well it's my favourite sweater. It's a comfort thing."

Her mom nodded. "Come on, dinner's ready."

CHAPTER 21

"She's here!" Barb called from the kitchen, setting the phone down. "I've just buzzed her through the security door."

By the time Molly made the walk from the elevator to Brandon's door he was waiting in the hallway. "I've got the old console set up so we can crash go-karts for a while," he grinned. "Unless you want to rock out instead, I can change the wires over.

"Go karts is fine," she said and stepped inside.

"Hiya honey!" Barb called. "I'm just baking. I'll bring some out to you when it's ready."

"Thanks, Barb," Molly said.

"Aren't you warm in that?" Brandon said.

Molly tucked her hands inside her sleeves of her sweater. "It's for comfort," she said, repeating the lie she had told her mother.

Brandon nodded and smiled softly at her. "The console is set up in the living room. Did you still want to play?"

She nodded again and forced a little smile because she knew the alternative was talking. She'd found it easier to smile these last few weeks but with the bandages on her wrists she didn't feel like smiling at all. She would have cancelled her "play date" –as Shannon was calling it – with Brandon but he would have asked too many questions or simply shown up at her house. So she was here, faking her smiles, and trying to act like she was still getting better.

Playing old video games with Brandon actually made her feel like she was getting better. It felt good to laugh, it felt good to be goofy-competitive with someone who didn't care if he won or lost, it felt good to relax and forget.

Barb, true to her word, brought down a heaping plate of warm chocolate chip cookies. "Don't tell your mom I fed you cookies for lunch."

Molly laughed because Barb had said the same thing whenever Molly came over as a child. She took a cookie and ate half in one bite.

"These are just as good as I remember," she said. It came out muffled by the mouth full of cookie.

Barb smiled back. "Don't eat yourself sick or we'll all be busted. Enjoy your afternoon! I'm going to pick up some groceries" She disappeared and for a while Brandon and Molly just sat back and enjoyed the warm chocolaty goodness of the cookies.

Molly was feeling so normal and so relaxed that when Brandon said; "Are you ready for a rematch?" she rolled up her sleeves and said, "Bring it on!"

For a moment she couldn't understand why his grin had disappeared. When it clicked in her mind she yanked her sleeves down and said, "Are we going to play or not?"

"What happened?"

"Nothing 'happened', okay? I don't want to talk about it, can we just play?"

"Let me see."

"Why? It's nothing."

He took her hands and pushed back her sleeves. He sat there for a long time, his eyes never leaving her wrists, her hands held firmly but gently in his so she couldn't hide what she had done. "Why did …"

"Why did I do it?" Molly snapped. "I get so tired of all of this sometimes. I get tired of fighting when no one wants me to win. I get tired of being alone. I get tired of no one liking me! I'm tired of pretending that I'm getting better so that everyone else will be happy with me! Well I tried to be better and it didn't work. I tried to be better and I ran straight in to Lance again and I couldn't handle it alone! Everyone thinks I should be better because I can eat supper in the kitchen every night but I'm not better!"

"Why didn't you call me if you were hurting so bad? I would have come over."

Molly swallowed hard. There was no accusation in his voice, only pain. "I'm sorry. I don't want to be a bother. I call you all the time, even in the middle of the night. I didn't want to bother you again."

"Molly, you're not a bother. You're healing and I want to help you. You can call me, any time, as often as you need to. You can talk to your mom and step-dad too but I understand if you feel you can't."

When Molly got home her parents were in the kitchen talking over coffee. Between her step-dad's long shifts and her mom working from home, they didn't often have that time together. Molly hesitated, not wanting to intrude, not wanting to be a bother.

"You're not a bother," she heard Brandon say in her head.

Taking a deep breath she managed to get as far as the kitchen doorway. They looked up at her. "Hi, Molly," her mom said, smiling. "How's Brandon?"

"Good. We talked a lot today."

"That's good. I know you're still seeing the psychologist once a week but it's good to have other people to talk to."

"I ... uh ... wanted to talk to you guys about something, if now's an okay time?"

"Of course," her step-dad said. "Anything you need."

Her smile was weak and faded too quickly. "I know I'm not hiding in my room anymore, but I'm still scared most of the time. I'm scared of a lot of things. I'm scared of going to school in the fall. I don't know how I'm supposed to face everyone. I ran into Julie at the store yesterday and ..."

Her mom nodded. "And now you're wearing a comfort sweater. I'll talk to the division about getting you transferred. There is a second high school in the area but it means no school bus."

"Oh, I don't want to inconvenience you. I know it's hard with the one car and ..."

Her step-dad set his coffee down on the table with a solid thump. "Molly, we'll make the driving work. If you can't go back to that school we'll find another way. You're not an inconvenience to us."

"Okay." It seemed like the right thing to say and she didn't want to argue with them. She didn't want to tell them she didn't believe them. She didn't want to hurt them or let them down.

"Thank-you for telling us," her mom said. "Whatever you need to help you feel safe we'll do our best to get for you. We love you."

"Yeah," she said automatically. "Okay Mom." She stepped back and fled to her room.

It was almost a week later and Molly hadn't given the school matter a second thought. Her wrists had healed enough that she could hide what she'd done with concealer instead of bandages which was easier since it meant she could wear short sleeves again. She snuck out of her room and made her way to the kitchen in search of a snack to tie her over until supper and ran straight into her mom who was coming out of the kitchen.

Molly's eyes dropped to the floor. "I'm sorry."

"Don't be. I was in such a rush I didn't see you. I was actually coming to find you."

"Why?"

"I just finished about an hour's worth of phone calls with different people at the school board. I've explained your situation and they said changing schools wouldn't be a problem."

"Oh. Right. I haven't really given it much thought. I wasn't sure what would happen."

Her mom smiled. "I thought that might be the case. They said you don't have to make a decision until the end of August."

Molly glanced up and forced a smile.

"I'm sorry; I'm still in your way." Her mom stepped back and let Molly into the kitchen.

When Molly looked over her shoulder her mom was already gone. She relaxed and let the smile drop from her face. It wasn't that she wasn't happy, only that being outwardly happy was still so much work and it still felt so fake.

But I don't have to worry about school anymore. I can just enjoy my summer. Or try to. That feels good.

It was one of those grey days that called for sweaters and hiding indoors so Molly and Brandon had the playground to themselves. The gravel crunched under their shoes as they headed for the swings. Brandon kicked his feet, swinging as high as he could but Molly just watched, her toes never leaving the dusty gravel.

When Brandon slowed to a stop he grinned at her. "I still like playgrounds," he said. "I just want to run around and climb everything again."

Molly shook her head. "I'd feel like a dork."

"Yea, I always feel like a dork when someone sees me do something like that. But it's still fun." After a moment he went on. "Sometimes you have to stop caring about what's cool and do what makes you happy."

"I don't know what makes me happy. Everything I do just makes more problems. Something is always going wrong."

"It can feel that way, but good things happen all the time too."

"Maybe to you."

"Good things happen to everybody, they're just harder to see, that's all."

Molly sighed. "Maybe you're right. You were always tripping over your words when you talked to me before, what happened?"

He smiled. "I don't know. I still feel like I don't make sense most of the time."

"I watched your presentation, you made sense then. You really sounded grown-up and important."

"Oh, I didn't think you'd actually watch that."

"Yeah, it was back when you yelled at me. That was why I deleted all those people. Did you really witness the fight between me and Lance?"

"Yeah, I was running an errand for my electronics teacher. I pulled my phone out and recorded it. I guess I should have told you."

"I would have been mad at you if you had told me."

"You're not mad that I did a project about you?"

Molly took a deep breath. "I'm embarrassed, but I'm not mad. It must have been a lot of work, changing projects at the last minute like that."

"Actually I changed projects to bullying when you dropped the class, I added on the suicide part after you ended up in the hospital. I had to make special arrangements with the teacher. I was the last one to present and I didn't have to hand in my report until the last day of exams. The day after, when the principal told the whole school, I watched all these people crying because they'd almost lost you and I knew they were the ones who had destroyed your life. I wanted to show everyone what they had done to you."

"Were they really upset that I had tried to kill myself?"

"They said they were but it was all an act."

The rain started without warning and sent them scrambling towards the play structure. There was only one platform big enough for them to hide under and it meant they both had to crouch but at least they were out of the downpour.

Molly was soaked through and she felt cold and miserable. When she looked at Brandon to complain he was grinning like a fool. "What's so funny?"

"We look like a couple of drowned cats!"

Molly chuckled. "I guess we do." Her phone rang. "Hold on, it's my mom. Hello?"

"Where are you?" her mom asked.

"I'm still at the park with Brandon."

"Isn't it raining there?"

"Yeah. We're hiding under the play structure. Maybe it will let up soon."

"I'll send your step-dad down with the car."

"I don't want to be a bother."

"It's no bother, Molly. We love you."

"Thanks Mom." She tucked the phone away. "My step-dad is coming to rescue us."

"At least we won't miss lunch!" His smile dropped. "You remember that … no of course you remember. I called you, when you were at the coffee shop, right? You had butt dialed me and I heard some of what Lance said and …"

"Brandon, why did you stick by me? I was a real bitch to you and you still came after me."

"Oh, well, we've been friends for so long and I didn't trust Kirsten or Lance, especially after you started changing so quickly, so I tried to look out for you without making you angry at me."

"Oh. I thought maybe it was because you, you know, liked me."

He shrugged. "I've never thought about it. Dating seems like a hassle."

"It is," Molly agreed.

"Isn't it nice just to be friends with no pressure or expectations?"

"Yeah. Sometimes you make me laugh and I wonder what it would be like if we were dating."

"Molly, I don't think that would be a good idea. I care, and I'll be there for you, but …"

"I know."

"I was about to make a fool of myself, wasn't I?"

"Probably. I don't think I'm ready to date again anyways." She sighed. "I told myself I wasn't going to ask this but I have to know. Have you heard anything about the girls?"

"Well, Kirsten is out of the hospital and getting better but that's all I know. She won't talk to me and we don't have any friends in common."

"Right."

"I saw Amanda around school those last few weeks and sometimes she comes into the music store. She's hanging out with some other girls I recognize from school but I couldn't tell you their names. She smiles at me but doesn't talk to me either."

"And Julie? She was dating Lance last I heard."

"Knocked up."

"Oh."

Brandon nudged her. "There's the car, come on."

They made a mad dash through the rain and piled into the back seat of the car. "Thanks for coming," Molly said.

"I'll always come," her step-dad replied. "We love you."

And for the first time in weeks Molly was starting to believe him.

EPILOGUE

Molly stood in front of the full length mirror in her mother's room twisting this way and that and occasionally fussing with a loose hair or a crooked seam. She had spent weeks going from store-to-store looking, sometimes with Brandon, or Shannon, or her mom, and sometimes on her own, looking for the perfect dress. On one of her alone trips she had come out of a mall boutique store feeling disappointed and had nearly walked into two boys about her age.

"Are you Molly?"

She looked from one to the other and recognized their sneers and the glint in their eyes. "Why?" she said; pulling out her phone.

"Are you free for a few hours? My friend and I heard you were good for a romp."

"And you are?"

"I'm Darryl and this is Phil."

"Well, Darryl and Phil, I just need to make a quick phone call." She pretended to dial and put the phone to her ear. "Hi, could you put me through to Detective Price? No, I'm fine but there are two boys here giving me a hard time again."

The boys bolted.

Molly smiled at the memory. It had been the first time in over a year that anyone had approached her with a sexual request and it was distressing that it might never go away, but she had wanted to call Dr. Jesse, whom she no longer saw, and tell him how well she had handled the situation on her own.

She heard the doorbell ring and forced herself to take a deep breath. She'd been just as nervous walking across the stage this morning knowing everyone was looking at her. She had turned and smiled, like she was supposed to, and spotted Shannon bouncing in the aisle cheering. Her smile became real then and she even waved at her little sister. The pretending to be normal was easier with Shannon.

"Molly," her mom called. "Brandon is here."

"These are applications papers to the local community college," her step-dad said.

"And a letter explaining your situation and recommending that they consider your application even though the deadline has passed," her mother added.

Shaking Molly held up the last item; a cheque for one hundred dollars.

"This is a personal cheque, Molly," her step-dad said. "This isn't from the school."

Molly carefully put everything back in the envelope and handed it to her mother. "I don't want it to get lost."

"We'll go over it tomorrow," her mom said, tucking it away in her purse.

When dinner was over the parents and siblings prepared to leave so the grads and their dates could enjoy their loud music until very late.

"What time do you want her home?" Brandon asked.

Molly's mom shrugged. "Whenever the party ends." She hugged Molly tight. "We're so proud of you, sweetie, and we love you so much."

And Molly believed it.

ABOUT THE AUTHOR

Casia Schreyer has been a stay-at-home mother for nearly three years but has recently returned to the working world. She lives in Southeastern Manitoba with her husband and two children. She reads and writes in many genres.

In addition to writing Casia enjoys knitting and crocheting, spending time with her family, and working in the yard.

Casia Schreyer can be reached online at the following links:
www.facebook.com/schreyerauthor
www.casiaschreyer.wordpress.com
@CasiaSchreyer

Made in the USA
Charleston, SC
21 November 2014